SO MUCH
IT HURTS

SO MUCH
IT HURTS

monique polak

ORCA BOOK PUBLISHERS

Library and Archives Canada Cataloguing in Publication

Polak, Monique
So much it hurts / Monique Polak.

Issued also in electronic format.
ISBN 978-1-4598-0136-3

I. Title.
PS8631.O43S6 2013   jc813'.6   C2013-901915-4

First published in the United States, 2013
Library of Congress Control Number: 2013935380

Summary: A teen actress gets involved with an older director, whose explosive temper
and controlling behavior threaten to destroy her life.

*Orca Book Publishers is dedicated to preserving the environment and
has printed this book on Forest Stewardship Council® certified paper.*

Orca Book Publishers gratefully acknowledges the support for its publishing programs
provided by the following agencies: the Government of Canada through the Canada Book
Fund and the Canada Council for the Arts, and the Province of British Columbia
through the BC Arts Council and the Book Publishing Tax Credit.

Cover design by Teresa Bubela
Cover image by iStockphoto.com
Author photo by Studio Iris/Monique Dykstra

ORCA BOOK PUBLISHERS   ORCA BOOK PUBLISHERS
PO Box 5626, STN. B   PO Box 468
VICTORIA, BC CANADA   CUSTER, WA USA
V8R 6S4   98240-0468

www.orcabook.com
Printed and bound in Canada.

16 15 14 13 • 4 3 2 1

For all the young women who see themselves in Iris,
and for the people who love them
and want to know them better

CHAPTER 1

"I have a daughter—have while she is mine..."
—*HAMLET,* ACT 2, SCENE 2

I can feel myself becoming Ophelia.

My shoulders drop, my face softens. The rows of orange lockers grow blurry, until they're not lockers anymore.

I'm in Elsinore, in Denmark, far away and long ago. I'm wandering outside the gray stone walls of the royal palace. The orange is the sun as it rises over the ramparts. I cross my hands over my heart.

I never knew my mother, who died when she gave birth to me, and yet, with every breath I take, I miss her. No wonder that my father, Polonius, and my brother, Laertes, have been my everything.

Until now.

Until him.

Until Hamlet.

"Hamlet!" I don't mean to say his name out loud. Or to moan.

It happens when I'm getting into character. What's weird is how much I like turning into somebody else. I think it's because being me isn't exactly fascinating.

I'm in grade eleven at Westwood. I study hard; I make honor roll every term. Sundays, I waitress at Scoops. I've got a sort-of boyfriend—sort-of since I'm not sure I want him. At home, it's just me and Mom. My father left the country when he and Mom split up. I was four. I haven't seen him since. All Mom will say is there are complicated reasons why he can't visit. I guess the most interesting thing about me is that more than anything, I want to be a professional actor. Most people I know (including my mom) think it's a terrible idea. They think I should have a Plan B. I say, why can't I have my Plan A?

If I had to sum up in one sentence what my dilemma is, the way a plot gets summed up on a Broadway playbill, here is what I'd say: *Iris Wagner is waiting for her life to begin.*

"I-ris, you total ditz!" When Katie nudges me, I nearly lose my balance, making me feel like even more of a ditz. "Are you talking to yourself again? Hey, I meant to ask you—did you do your chemistry homework?"

What Katie really means is will I let her copy my assignment. Katie is not the academic type. She's more the clubbing type.

I can't believe how much makeup she's wearing today. Her eyes are rimmed in purple pencil, her eyelids are smoky gray, and her lips are glossier than her patent clutch. She signed up for Theater Workshop too, but only because it means she can do makeup—and because it lets her start school late on Fridays. Thursday is ladies' night at the clubs on Crescent Street (which means ladies—even underage ones with fake IDs—get in free). Katie needs Friday mornings to recover.

We have Theater Workshop in the basement at Westwood, just past the lockers. Our theater teacher, Ms. Cameron, helped design the space. The acoustics are amazing, and there's a giant wooden stage with state-of-the-art lighting and thick plum-colored velvet curtains that *swish* when they open. That *swish* is one of the reasons I want to be an actor.

That *swish* means the show is about to begin—and I love beginnings. Beginnings of movies, of books, of meals. Beginnings are when everything is possible, when nothing's gone wrong yet. It's middles and endings I have trouble with.

I tried explaining this to my mom the other night, but she didn't get it. "You want to become an actor because you like the sound the velvet curtains make?" She shook her head. "It's one thing to follow your heart, Iris—not that following my heart worked out too well for me—but in this day and age, a person needs to be practical. You don't want to keep working in that ice-cream parlor for the rest of your life, do you? And chances are, if you really do try to become a professional actor, that's where you'll end up— waitressing between auditions. I'm not saying you should give up acting or that you're not talented. Acting can always be your hobby, Iris."

The other students are filing into Theater Workshop now too. There's Lenore, who's playing Gertrude. It's a bigger role than mine, but Gertrude's a bitch (so's Lenore, making her perfect for the part). I like Ophelia way better. Ophelia has soul. She cares about people and she loves with all her heart. She'd never get it on with her sleazy brother-in-law the way Gertrude did.

Lenore's with Antoine, Katie's ex, whom Katie no longer speaks to. "He's dead to me," she said after they broke up. She slid the back of her hand across her forehead. For someone who's not into Theater Workshop, Katie can be quite dramatic. Behind them is Tommy, the boyfriend I don't think I want.

Tommy waves. I feel obliged to wave back. When he realizes we haven't left him room on the bench, his shoulders slump. Which makes him look sad. Which makes me feel guilty. Which makes me think I definitely don't want him for a boyfriend. Not now. Not ever. Even if he is nice—and decent-looking. Even if Mom approves.

If we're taking notes in Theater Workshop, we sit on the stadium benches where the audience sits during performances. Luckily, there isn't much theory. We don't even use a textbook. Ms. Cameron believes in what she calls the "experiential approach," which means we mostly do on-the-spot exercises and rehearse. Ms. Cameron says people learn more from their own experience than they do from books.

Ms. Cameron has someone with her today. A lanky guy with a soul patch is watching us from the corner of the room. I like how he's dressed—gray fedora, gray plaid shirt and skinny black jeans. When his eyes land on me, I straighten my back. I know my posture sucks. When the visitor's gaze shifts to someone else, I feel disappointed.

Ms. Cameron is about thirty. She was a child actress, and she still has many friends who are actors. The lanky guy is probably an actor too, though I don't recognize him. Maybe he's from the Concordia University theater program, or he could be a drama specialist from out of town. Ms. Cameron won a prize for excellence in teaching, and visitors sometimes come to watch her work. I guess she's still performing, even if she gave up acting long ago to become a theater teacher.

Katie says Ms. Cameron must've peaked when she was ten, and her career went south after that. I hate when Katie badmouths Ms. Cameron.

Ms. Cameron claps. "Today," she says, "I want you to slap yourselves."

I'm not sure I've heard right, but then Ms. Cameron repeats herself. "Slap yourselves."

"You sure that's a good idea, Ms. C?" Antoine calls out.

"Of course it's a good idea, Antoine. They're the only kind I get." Ms. Cameron throws her head back when she laughs—and I notice her exchange a look with the guest. "Well then, go ahead," she says, turning back to us. "Use both hands. Start with your foreheads and cheeks; make your way down to your toes."

Ms. Cameron closes her eyes to demonstrate. Leave it to Ms. Cameron to make slapping herself look sexy. As usual, her long blond hair is tied back in a ponytail, and she's wearing all black—black tank top, black tights and a slinky black skirt. When she slaps herself, it's like she's playing drums, only the drums are her body. "This is a marvelous way to get the blood flowing," she says, her eyes still closed.

At first, there's some laughter—this happens a lot during Ms. Cameron's warm-ups, and then we all (even Antoine) start slapping ourselves. My body bristles at the first slap, but I'm careful not to slap myself too hard. Soon I feel my body waking up, coming to life in a way I'm not used to.

I don't feel like Ophelia. But I don't feel like Iris either. I feel more like…like Ms. Cameron. Sexy. Confident. Grown up.

I don't know where Ms. Cameron gets all her ideas. She never uses the same warm-up twice.

"Now," Ms. Cameron says, "I want you to find a partner and take turns slapping each other. Gently. We never hurt each other in Theater Workshop—or anywhere else." Her eyes meet the visitor's again.

Katie shimmies over. "Hey, partner." She lowers her voice. "I came to save you from Tommy. You owe me. You can repay me in chemistry assignments." When Katie raises her hand to slap me, I back away. That cracks her up. "What do you think I'm going to do?" she asks. "Beat up my bestie?"

"Let's keep things serious, please," Ms. Cameron calls out. "Fingertips only. No palms."

Katie must not know her own strength, because the whack she gives me makes my cheek smart. "Hey," I say, rubbing the skin, "that hurt!"

Katie brings her hand to her mouth. "Yikes, Iris. Sorry. I swear I didn't mean it. You get me back now, okay?" She turns to me, closes her eyes and grins.

She knows I'd feel awful if I hurt her. I'd feel awful if I hurt anyone. I'm the kind of person who'd rather scoop a spider up in a napkin and carry him outside than flush him down the toilet. Slapping Katie is even harder for me than getting slapped.

"Who's that guy in the corner?" Katie whispers.

7

"How should I know?"

"He's seriously hot."

"People!" Ms. Cameron claps again. "Now that you're warmed up, I'd like to introduce a friend of mine. This is Mick Horton."

Mick Horton gives us a businesslike nod; then he turns to Ms. Cameron and nods at her too, like he's giving her permission to continue. "Mick is an award-winning stage director in Melbourne, Australia, and he's come to Montreal to consult on a project here. He's kindly agreed to sit in on our class today."

Katie leans in close to me. "D'you think Mick and Ms. Cameron are getting it on?"

"How should I know?"

Mick Horton sits on a tall stool, watching as we start rehearsal. Is it my imagination or does he have a permanent scowl on his face?

Ms. Cameron wants us to do some work on the end of Act 1, Scene 3. Which is where Ophelia comes in. Drop shoulders, soften face. It's time for my Ophelia mind-meld.

I feel Mick Horton's eyes on me as I say my lines. I don't know if it's because he thinks I'm talented—or terrible. Terrible, probably.

Polonius is rattling on and on the way Polonius does. He criticizes Ophelia for giving her heart too easily to

Hamlet—he says she has not placed a high enough value on herself. *Tender yourself more dearly,* he tells her. Poor Ophelia—stuck with such a depressing windbag for a father. *Do not believe his vows,* he warns her, and then he orders Ophelia to keep away from the Danish prince!

I would not, in plain terms, from this time forth,
Have you so slander any moment leisure,
As to give words or talk with the Lord Hamlet.
Look to't, I charge you.

I bow my head. Ms. Cameron is always telling us to draw on our deepest feelings to bring our performances alive. I think about how my father's not around to warn me against guys he doesn't like. I know what it feels like to miss a father. So I take that feeling and try to find the love inside. How much I'd love my father if I only knew him! How torn apart I'd be if he told me Lord Hamlet was no good for me. Because I love the Danish prince with every fiber of my being.

"'I shall obey, my lord,'" I say—I mean, Ophelia says. Only it's both of us speaking, me and Ophelia in one breath.

When I look up, Mick Horton is still watching me.

"Nice work today, people," Ms. Cameron calls out when the bell rings.

"That was deeply felt, Iris," she says when I pass her. "Fine work—as usual."

9

Mick Horton is standing next to her. His nose is too big for his narrow face. Still, Katie's right—there is something hot about him. Something magnetic. I can't help hoping he and Ms. Cameron are not getting it on.

Then Mick Horton does something I'd never have expected. He plants his hand on my shoulder. His fingers are long and slender, like a pianist's; his touch is cool and dry, but something about it makes me feel privileged. I have the feeling he's a person who keeps his distance, and yet he is not keeping it with me.

"The way you slouch," he says, looking right at me (he has the darkest eyes I've ever seen), "works for Ophelia. Especially when she's submitting to her father. But you should do something with your hair. Comb it away from your face."

Katie is next to me, but we don't say a word till we're outside the theater room. "I can't believe he said that about your hair! I love your hair! The guy's got some nerve. You shoulda told him that soul patch looks like pubes."

CHAPTER 2

"Lord Hamlet is a prince, out of thy star;
This must not be." —HAMLET, ACT 2, SCENE 2

A family of four sits down at one of my tables. I grab two menus and some crayons. When I get to the table, I look at the mom, avoiding direct eye contact with the dad. Parents want crayons for their kids. Crayons keep kids occupied and, with a little luck, quiet. And even if it's usually Dad who leaves the tip, a waitress who makes too much eye contact with him risks being considered by Mom to be flirting with her husband—adversely affecting the tip.

Waitressing is just another role I play—one I happen to be very good at. Sundays from twelve to six, I become a cheerful, charming and efficient waitress. I greet every customer with a smile, put others' needs before my own and take pleasure in my life of service.

At the end of each shift, my apron's heavier than the shield they make me wear at the dentist's office when they x-ray my teeth. Only my apron pockets are filled with coins and bills, not lead.

Four months of working here and I could write a book about tipping.

I worked full-time over the summer. I wasn't planning to keep working once school started, but the manager, Phil, is flexible about my hours. He gives me time off when I'm performing. "I know it's important to support the arts, Iris. A person's gotta have balance. A person can't think *business business business* all the time." That's what Phil told me when we were working out my schedule. He's a decent guy, even if he's a little too into speechifying. I'm also used to the tips. Mom's decluttering business is doing okay now, but she still has to be careful with money, and this way, I don't need to ask for spending money.

On the other hand, there are some things I really hate about this job. Number one: my uniform. It's supposed to be retro, but even when I try thinking of it as a costume, I still despise it. It's a brown-and-white-checked blouse with short puffy sleeves, and over the blouse is an awful brown apron-dress made of scratchy polyester. The shoes are worse, and though we get the uniform for free, we actually have to buy the shoes. They're the kind nurses wear—thick white leather with white leather laces and gray crepe soles that stick to the floor, especially after some kid has spilled his milkshake.

I open my order pad to a fresh page. "Have you ever tried our bubblegum ice cream?" I ask the two kids, who are already drawing on their place mats.

"Bubblegum!" The two kids look up from their masterpieces.

The little girl is the spitting image of her dad. Same wavy red hair. She doesn't notice when her brother takes one of her crayons and adds it to his pile.

The mom looks up at me, smiling. I can tell she feels sorry for me that I have to wear such an ugly uniform.

I take a quick look at what the kids have drawn on their place mats. The girl has made a giant purple blotch. Jackson Pollock, pre-K period. It's hard to know if what is on the boy's place mat is a house or an elephant. "Cool drawings!" I tell them.

The family's good for a five-dollar tip. More if the kids like the ice cream and the girl doesn't figure out her brother nicked her crayon.

Scoops has a long, narrow entrance, so I usually notice when someone walks in. But I must've been distracted by the kids' drawings, because somehow, as if by magic, Mick Horton is sitting at the counter in the middle of the restaurant. I have to look twice to be sure it's him. But I already know it is. I feel his presence, the way I did in Theater Workshop.

Something about him makes me tremble inside. Maybe it's because he's Ms. Cameron's friend and I look up to her so much. Or because he's so well known in the theater world. I googled him after class, and I swear I got five hundred hits. Apparently, he's known as the *enfant terrible* of the Australian theater scene. How cool is that? And he's won a ton of prizes and traveled to theater festivals around the world.

I feel myself blush when I look at him. Thank God he doesn't know I've been stalking him online. He's stroking his soul patch. I can't believe Katie said it looks like pubes. I think the soul patch makes him look artistic.

"Uh, Mr. Horton, right?" I say when I walk to the other side of the counter and hand him his menu. I hope he doesn't notice my hands are shaking.

I feel his eyes on my fingers. When I look up at him, he's smiling, but just a little. The smile makes him look younger. He's wearing the fedora again and a different pair of skinny jeans, this time with a white T-shirt.

He lays the menu facedown on the counter. "How 'bout calling me Mick? 'Mr. Horton' makes me think people are talking to my granddad. You're Iris, right?"

I'm so surprised he knows my name that for a second I'm afraid I'm going to trip over my ugly shoes.

"Isobel said you worked here," he says, as if it's the most natural thing in the world that an internationally acclaimed theater director would care where I worked.

"Iso—?" I start to ask, then realize he means Ms. Cameron. "Do you…uh…know what you want?"

The question makes him grin. I feel my cheeks get hot again.

"What a guy like me wants…now that's a complicated question. Existential even. But right now, what I really want is a scoop of vanilla ice cream. Dish, no cone."

I don't say what I usually do when people order vanilla, that we have sixty-one other flavors and double mocha fudge is my personal favorite. I'm too nervous to say any of that.

"I have to tell you, Iris, I didn't just come for ice cream," Mick Horton says. (I can't call him just Mick, not even in my head.) "I came because I want you to know I think you've got a great deal of potential." He pauses, and I get the feeling he likes the word *potential.* "As an actress. I'm looking forward to helping you develop that potential."

"Wow," I say, and my order pad slips out of my hand and falls to the floor. I lean over to pick it up, and I can feel his eyes on me again. He's checking me out. I know he is. But it's more than that. He's looking at me—gazing at me—as if he can see inside me too. I like how that feels. "That…that's amazing," I manage to say. "It means so much—coming from someone like you. Someone so…" I let the end of my sentence drop. What was I going to say? Someone so famous? Someone so hot?

I'm saved by a customer calling from the front of the restaurant. "Miss, can I get a little more water over here, please?"

"I'll bring you that scoop of vanilla straightaway," I tell him.

The banana split I've ordered for another table is ready. I can bring the water at the same time. Then the family's order, then the scoop of vanilla. Sometimes, waitressing is like being an air traffic controller.

The customer who wants more water is an older woman who's been reading the Saturday paper. She doesn't look at me when I fill her glass. To her, I am just a waitress. I wish I could tell her I'm not. I push my shoulders back. Mick Horton thinks I have *a great deal of potential.* As an actress.

CHAPTER 3

"The time is out of joint..."
—*HAMLET,* ACT 1, SCENE 5

I shouldn't be here. I shouldn't be doing this.

Not letting him take off my T-shirt or run his fingers along the outside of my jeans, pressing harder when he gets near my thighs.

I don't even *want* to be doing this. Not really. But it's not just him moaning—it's me too. Now that I'm here doing this, I can't just make it stop.

"I love you, Iris," Tommy says as he pulls his T-shirt over his head. His chest is narrow and his nipples are hard brown acorns.

Tommy's parents have gone to New York for the weekend and taken his little sister with them. He has the house to himself. When I said I'd come over tonight, I knew what I was agreeing to.

Tommy and I have spent whole nights making out, usually at my house, in the basement with the door open (Mom's rule), but not doing *it*. The way we are about to now.

I know Tommy expects me to say I love him back. I feel guilty for not saying it. But I can't. Because I've never been more sure that I *don't* love him.

It's my first time, but not Tommy's. He told me he had sex with a girl last summer when they were both working at a camp in the Laurentians. Even if I don't love Tommy, I can't help feeling a little jealous of that girl.

"Are you sure you want to?" Tommy whispers, even though there's no one around to hear us. We're lying on his bed. The walls in his room are covered with vintage *Star Wars* posters. He stretches out his arm to reach for something. It takes me a second to realize he's got condoms in the top drawer of his nightstand. He must've known—or at least hoped—this was going to happen.

"I'm sure," I tell him, though I'm not.

Tommy makes a gasping sound. He's still got his jeans on too, and I can feel how excited he is. How much he wants this to happen.

I'm seventeen. That's two years older than Katie was the first time she had sex. I'm sick of waiting. I'm sick of feeling like some kid. And it's not like Tommy's using me, the way a lot of guys our age use girls for sex. Tommy really cares about me.

"It can hurt the first time." His voice is shaky. "I don't want to hurt you, Iris."

"I'll be fine." Why am I the one reassuring him?

Tommy is standing up now, kicking off his jeans and white boxers. I've never seen a naked guy with an erection before, and the sight of Tommy standing there makes me want to laugh. He looks so…so funny. Almost like some cartoon character.

I don't think a girl is supposed to feel like laughing the first time she has sex.

The whole thing happens so quickly, I can hardly keep track of the steps that come between following Tommy into his bedroom and doing *it*. When I start taking off my clothes, Tommy says, "No, I want to do it." His excitement adds to my own. My mind may not be sure that this is the right thing to do, but my body's not arguing. "Mmm," I hear myself say when Tommy runs his fingers across my belly.

Tommy's hands are shaking. He's nervous, too, even if this isn't his first time. Knowing that makes me feel bad for him.

I want to ask Tommy to slow down, but there isn't time, and besides, I don't think he could. And then, too quickly, it's over. His eyes are closed now, and he's got this blissed-out Buddha look on his face. His forehead's sweaty, and when some sweat beads land in the space between my breasts,

I untuck one of my hands from behind his neck to wipe the sweat away.

If I loved him, I wouldn't mind his sweat on me.

It did hurt, the way everyone says it does when a girl has sex the first time, but the pain was sharp and over quickly. Now, my belly feels as tender as on the first day of my period.

There is a spot of brownish blood on the sheet.

"You okay, Iris?"

I should tell him about the blood. He'll have to wash the sheets before his parents get home. "I'm fine."

I'm afraid he's going to tell me again that he loves me. But that isn't what he says. "Did it hurt?"

"Nah."

"Did you...like it?" I know what Tommy means is did I come. I know all about coming—Katie is obsessed with orgasms (she says she once had three in one night with Antoine)—but I'm pretty sure I didn't have one. From what Katie says, it's the kind of thing you can't miss.

I give Tommy my best smile. "Yeah, sure," I tell him. "Sure I liked it."

The main thing is, I'm not sorry we did it. Not one bit. Tommy's a decent guy. And, well, at least I've gotten it over with.

"Let's just rest," I tell Tommy. "And not talk."

He wraps one arm around my shoulders. I close my eyes.

When I do, I am startled by what I see in my head. Not Tommy, not his vintage posters, not his white boxer shorts crumpled on the carpet. My mind's not even in this room.

In my imagination, I see someone else.

Mick Horton. His fedora hangs low over his forehead, and he's smirking at me. It's as if he knows exactly what I've just done.

CHAPTER 4

"...she would hang on him
As if increase of appetite had grown
By what it fed on..." —HAMLET, ACT 1, SCENE 2

It's ironic that my mom owns the Clear Your Clutter Closet Company (try saying that quickly five times in a row!). She goes around Montreal organizing other people's closets. She tells customers what to throw out and what to keep; then she draws up elaborate plans to redesign their closet space. Deep shelves for sweaters, low shelves for shoes, taller ones for boots. Mom charges a hundred dollars an hour. What's ironic is that our closets are a disaster. Open any one and expect to be struck by an avalanche. "Don't mention it to people, Iris. Not even as a joke," Mom says. "It could be bad for business."

It doesn't help that I collect clothes. It drives Mom crazy that I shop mostly in the vintage shops along Mount Royal Avenue. Mom insists that everything I bring home either gets hung out on our clothesline or, when it's too cold for that, spun in the hot dryer for two cycles. "Those old rags could be crawling with bedbugs. If we had a bedbug infestation, Iris, and people found out—it would destroy my business. And where would that leave us?"

The Clear Your Clutter Closet Company has been supporting us for as long as I can remember. My father isn't able to send money. Mom won't say why that is. When I was younger, I sometimes asked about him, but she always got a stomachache or headache, so I stopped. When you only have one parent, the last thing you want is for her to get sick. The only thing I know for sure is that my dad had problems with money. That's why we lived in a cramped apartment for so many years before Mom saved enough to buy the house we live in now. It's also why my dad left Canada—and why he can't come back to visit.

Though Mom and I have always been pretty tight (we've had to be), there are certain things she doesn't get about me. Like why I'm so into theater and vintage clothes. Now, as I push on the door of Second Life, my favorite vintage shop, I feel the familiar rush. It's not just the smell of lavender and mothballs. It's the feeling that I'm on the hunt, that I could be seconds away from the fashion find of a lifetime, the perfect skirt or dress or pair of capris—the outfit that'll transform me into the Iris I was meant to be.

I recognize the salesgirl. Julie has huge Marilyn Monroe-style platinum-blond hair and she's wearing a royal-blue cocktail dress with a sweetheart neckline.

"Hey, Iris." She looks up from her copy of *Vogue* (it's probably from the stack of old magazines near the cash register). "You picked a great day to come by. A woman came in yesterday with two bags full of stuff—skirts and dresses from the fifties. They belonged to her mom. And she must've been about your size."

Julie doesn't say whether the daughter is selling her mom's old clothes because the mom is dead. Some people get grossed out by the idea of wearing a dead person's clothes. I like it. Sometimes I swear I can feel a woman's spirit in her clothes, and by wearing them, it's as if I'm somehow keeping that spirit alive.

Julie's unpacked one bag. Because I'm a regular, she lets me unpack the second bag with her. The clothes haven't even been priced. I fall in love with the first thing I see—a short, sleeveless, black velvet dress. Julie notices me eyeing it. "It's going to look amazing on you. Try it on!"

I'm in the dressing room, zipping up, when the bell attached to the front door jingles. "Hi, how you doing?" Julie asks.

"Okeydokey. How 'bout you?"

It isn't only the Australian accent that's familiar. It's also the casual, confident way he's just asked, "How 'bout you?" What's Mick Horton doing here?

Julie laughs in a way that I know means she thinks Mick's hot. There's a pair of black high heels in the dressing room. They're a couple of sizes too big, but I slip them on and make my exit, being careful not to totter. The last thing I want right now is to look like a little girl playing dress-up.

"So what do you think?" I do a small spin in front of the floor-length mirror.

It doesn't occur to me until afterward that Mick isn't surprised to see me.

"Oh my god," Julie says, covering her mouth, "it's so you."

Which is exactly what I want when I try on clothes. For them to be me. Maybe because I'm still not sure who *me* is.

"Hey, Iris." I feel Mick's eyes on my face, then moving down the length of the dress, pausing at my chest, then at my hips. "Very elegant," he says. "Way better than those silly purple tights you were wearing the other day."

My cheeks get hot when Mick makes the comment about my purple tights. I got those tights on sale at H&M before school started. Usually, wearing them makes me happy, but now I make a mental note to dump them in the donation bin outside the Salvation Army store on Sherbrooke Street. Mick's right. They're silly. What was I thinking when I bought them?

"You two know each other?" Julie sounds impressed.

"Mr. Horton's working with—" He shakes his head when I call him Mr. Horton. I remember—too late—how he's told me to call him Mick. "I mean…Mick is working with our theater class."

"Wow, that's totally cool. Are you a director or something?" she asks Mick.

"Yeah, I've directed a few things." I like that he's so modest.

"Mick's famous," I tell Julie. Of course, I don't mention my online search.

Julie tells me the dress would normally sell for forty dollars, but that I can have it for thirty. "I mean, you're one of our best customers."

"That's great. Thanks so much, Julie."

I'm reaching for my wallet when Mick slaps two twenty-dollar bills down on the counter. "I want to buy that dress for you," he says. His eyes are dark pools.

"No way," I say, shaking my head and looking away because I'm too embarrassed to keep looking right at him. "I can't let you do that. It wouldn't be right."

"But I want to. It would make me happy. And you want to make me happy, don't you, Iris?"

"I do. Of course I do. It…it just doesn't seem right. Besides, I'm not used to someone treating me to things."

Mick pushes my hand back into my purse. His touch isn't what I expect. Not gentle but forceful, strong. Grown up. "Maybe it's time you started getting used to it."

It's Julie who ends up deciding for me. "Let him," she hisses. "Just say yes and enjoy your present."

So I do.

Mick wants to check out the men's hats. He tells me his fedora is vintage. He also says that though he's used to working with costume designers, he's always looking for interesting clothing his actors can wear onstage. "Vintage shops are a bit of an obsession for me," he tells us.

"You and Iris both," Julie says. Later, when he isn't looking, she winks at me.

Most of the men's hats are displayed on a pair of coat racks at the back of the shop. Julie says there are more in a box in the stockroom. When she goes to get the box, Mick and I check out the other hats. "You'd look good in that one," I say, pointing to a faded gray cowboy hat.

When Mick removes his fedora, I notice his hairline is receding. It's the only thing about him that makes him look older. He must notice me noticing because he pops on the cowboy hat. "What do you say?" he asks me.

"You look like a cowboy." What I'm really thinking is that he looks like a super hot Australian cowboy.

Mick makes me try on a pink pillbox hat. Its lacy veil covers my face. He shakes his head when I model it for him. "A face like yours shouldn't be covered."

"I'm also interested in vintage children's clothes. You don't carry any, do you?" Mick asks Julie when we've checked out all the hats.

I look at him when he says that. Something feels as if it's caught in my throat. It hadn't occurred to me that Mick might have a kid. Or that, for all I know, he might be married.

Mick must know what I'm thinking. "I have a little boy back home in Melbourne. His name is Nial. He's nearly two."

"Oh," I say, "that's great." I keep my voice bright, happy-sounding. Theater Workshop has made me good at pretending.

I can feel Mick watching my face. "His mom and I are separated. We have been since Nial was a year old."

"Oh, I'm sorry." Can Mick tell I'm lying?

"How 'bout a lift home?" he asks when the bell on the door jingles behind us.

"That'd be great." I'm trying to get into character. I don't want to come off like some goofy schoolgirl who's run into her crush. I want to be a sophisticated young woman out for a walk on Mount Royal Avenue with a sophisticated man. Because the sidewalk is crowded,

I have to move closer to Mick. For a split second, the outsides of our hands touch. I swear I can feel the fine hairs on the back of his hand. Oh my god.

"Do you have time for a coffee?" Mick asks.

I can't believe Mick Horton has just bought me a dress and now he's asking me to go for coffee! Talk about out of my league. Mick Horton is out of my solar system. The bag with my new old dress in it slips out of my hands. I'm not doing a very good job of playing a sophisticated young woman. Mick leans down to pick up the bag. The skin around his eyes crinkles when he laughs. "Am I making you nervous, Iris?"

"Uh, a little." There doesn't seem to be any point in lying.

"I'm going to take that as a good sign. A great sign. Come on, let's get a coffee. Isobel's always going on about how great the coffee in this city is." He makes getting a coffee sound like a weekend in Vegas.

I shift my shoulders back. Being with Mick makes me feel grown up. I like the feeling.

I feel the same when we get to the café and he pulls my chair out for me and insists on going to the counter for our lattes. "Aussie men are a little old-fashioned. I hope that's all right with you."

"I like it." Is that me—flirting with Mick? He laughs, and I nearly tell him about Tommy and how nervous he gets when he's around me.

I watch Mick as he stands in line, his hands thrust into the pockets of his jeans. The front of the café is all windows—garage-door style—and the sun is streaming in, lighting Mick up as if he's some kind of sun god.

I feel a woman at the next table watching me watch Mick. I give him a little wave, and he waves back. I want her to know we're together.

"Here's yours, gorgeous." Mick hands me my latte.

I take a sip and peer at him over the edge of my cup. He's left just the right amount of stubble over his upper lip. I want to ask him if he really thinks I'm gorgeous, but I'm afraid of sounding insecure.

"You really are gorgeous," he says. "But you don't think so, do you?" He doesn't wait for an answer. "It makes you even more gorgeous."

"Maybe I'm not used to compliments."

"We'll work on that," he says. " Hey, do you want to see a picture of my boy?"

"Sure. Does he look like you?"

"You tell me."

I'm expecting Mick to show me a photo on his cell phone, but instead he reaches into his back pocket and fishes out his wallet.

He comes to sit on my side of the booth. There isn't much room, so the side of his thigh presses against mine. It feels amazing.

He shows me a picture of a blond boy grinning into the camera. The boy is wearing faded denim overalls and a checkered shirt. His nose and cheeks are dusted with freckles.

It's only when I look more closely at the photograph that I notice something's missing. The photograph has been cut, but not just so it'll fit into the plastic sleeve inside Mick's wallet. No, someone's been cut out of the photograph. The cut marks are jagged. I don't have to ask who's missing from the photograph. It must be Nial's mother—Mick's wife.

And Mick's the one who cut her out.

CHAPTER 5

*"He hath, my lord, of late made many tenders
Of his affection to me."* —HAMLET, ACT 1, SCENE 3

I can't believe how easy it is to talk to Mick. Easier, even,
than talking to Katie. Katie's fun and we've been friends
since kindergarten, but we're really different. She thinks I
put too much energy into school and Theater Workshop
when I could be out at the clubs with her. I think she likes
making me feel she's cooler and more mature than I am.

Mick stays next to me on the banquette. I love how he
watches my face. He's interested in everything I say and
think. When I tell him I can barely remember my dad
and how my mom won't talk about him, Mick squeezes
my hand. "That must've been rough—growing up without
a dad. Especially for a little joey."

"A joey?" The word makes me laugh.

"I keep forgetting you're not an Aussie," Mick says.
"A joey is a baby kangaroo."

"I've never heard that word before."

"How do you like it?" I know he means the word *joey*, but it also feels like a bigger question—like he wants to know if I like being here with him.

"I like it. A lot."

Mick takes off his fedora and rubs his forehead. When he catches me watching him, he puts the fedora back on. I think it's cute that he's self-conscious about his hairline. Mick says he understands what things must have been like for me. He was seventeen when his father died of a heart attack. Mick says that before he got into directing, when he was in acting school in Melbourne, he used to summon up the grief he felt after his father's death. "I used that grief—that sense I'd been abandoned. I found a way to transform it into something else. You'll do that too, Iris. You've already begun doing it."

When Mick says that, it's as if something buried inside me starts to come to life again. There's a stirring in my chest. I've felt the same way as Mick—abandoned. Why hasn't my father tried to stay in touch with me all these years? Can he have forgotten his own daughter's existence?

I want Mick to know how much what he's just said matters to me, so I say, "I guess I always felt kind of sorry for myself. For not knowing my father the way other k— " I stop myself from saying *kids*. I don't want Mick to think of me that way. "The way other people do.

33

What you just said...it really means a lot. It makes me think that, in a way, the stuff I've gone through has had a purpose. Maybe I can summon that grief...that sense of being abandoned...and transform it into something else." It's only after I say those words that I realize they're the very same ones Mick just used. He doesn't seem to think that's a bad thing. He just nods and smiles, as if I've said something really deep.

"You know what, Iris?" he says when we finally get up to leave the café. "Being with you makes me feel everything is possible." He takes my hand, then lets it go, as if he's changed his mind and decided that holding my hand isn't the best idea. "You make me feel like a kid again." I can still feel the cool dry touch of his fingers. I want him to hold my hand and not let go this time.

"You're not old, Mick," I say, dropping my voice.

"I feel old. Compared to you."

Except for two worry lines—small train tracks—over the bridge of his nose, Mick's face is smooth. Only his hairline and his eyes hint that he's a lot older than me. When I look into his eyes, I can feel he's been through a lot. Felt a lot. Seeing that makes me feel closer to him. Is this what falling in love feels like? I know I've never felt this way around Tommy.

"How old do you think I am?" Now Mick's tone is playful, teasing.

I've never been good at guessing anyone's age. I don't want to say the wrong thing. "Well, you've got a kid. So you must be at least...I don't know..." I do the math in my head. "Twenty-two."

My guess makes Mick laugh. "Twenty-two? That would be sweet." But he doesn't say how old he is.

"I could take the metro," I tell Mick when he offers again to drive me home.

Mick insists. He's staying in a furnished loft in an apartment building a few blocks from where Mom and I live. He's also rented a Jeep with a camo paint job. He comes over to my side to help me step up into it. Again, he takes my hand, but only for a few seconds.

Maybe driving super slow is another Aussie thing. The closer he gets to my street, the more slowly Mick goes. The Jeep has a stick shift, so he needs both hands to drive. "Do you drive a Jeep in Melbourne too?"

"Yup. And always a stick. You get more control with a stick. Which I happen to enjoy. A lot."

"You don't have to take me to the door," I say when he's turning the corner to our street. It's not just that I don't want him going out of his way. It's also that I'm not sure how my mom would feel if she happened to be looking out the window and saw Mick and me together.

Mick doesn't ask me to explain. He pulls the Jeep over to the side of the road. When he puts his hand on mine,

I swear I can feel his pulse in his fingers. It's like I'm holding his heart. "I know this might sound crazy," he says, "but I really want to get to know you better, Iris."

"It doesn't sound crazy," I manage to say.

"Maybe we could have dinner sometime?"

"That'd be—" Something catches in my throat. Me, having dinner with this totally cool, totally hot guy? "—awesome."

I notice more crinkly lines around Mick's eyes when he smiles. They suit him.

"This Friday, then. Eight PM. I'll meet you here," he says, looking up at the house where he's stopped. Mick's not asking me; he's telling me. I like the way he takes charge, the way he wants to look after me.

"Okay." I don't want to move my hand away. Ever.

That's when I realize I want Mick to kiss me. Really kiss me. I wonder if he can tell that too. If he does, he doesn't do anything about it.

He's the one to take his hand away first. "One more thing," he calls out as I step out of the car. His voice has turned a little gruff, making it even sexier. "Let's not tell anyone about this, Joey. Got that?" Again, it's not a question.

"Got it. And thanks so much for the dress. Really, Mick, you shouldn't have."

What is it about Mick's telling me—warning me, really—not to tell anyone about us that bothers me?

It doesn't make any sense. I'm the one who didn't want him dropping me off in front of my house. Besides, who would I tell? Katie would never believe me.

I don't want to think about that. I want to think about how amazing Mick's hand felt on mine. And I want to imagine what it would be like to kiss him. The thought is so delicious and distracting that for a second I lose my footing and nearly fall off the sidewalk.

CHAPTER 6

"Seek for thy noble father in the dust."
—*HAMLET*, ACT 1, SCENE 2

I t's a go-go-go kind of day. We have two quizzes—one in Cal, one in World History. I spend recess sitting cross-legged in front of my locker, reviewing my notes on World War I. "You've got to be kidding," Katie says when she sees me.

The extra studying pays off. I can answer every question on the history quiz. "I guessed half of them," Katie tells me when we leave the exam room.

After classes are over, we go straight to rehearsal. Mick is there, scribbling notes. He looks up when I come into the room, and when our eyes meet, he smiles, but so quickly I'm not really sure it happened.

After that, I make a point of not looking at him. It's hard to do. It's even harder to believe that in forty-eight hours we'll be having dinner together. Me, Iris Wagner, with Mick Horton! I've already planned my outfit: the dress he bought me, black opaque tights, and my clunky black boots with the wedge heels. I'll wear my hair away from my face. I've been wearing it that way ever since Mick said I should. Mick has a great eye for detail. Theater directors have to notice everything.

I get home that afternoon before Mom. She phones from the car to say she went for coffee with a friend but that she's bringing home pizza from the Italian bakery and could I set the table.

The pizza is half pepperoni (for Mom), half tomato-and-mushroom (for me). "Come sit with me on the couch for a bit," Mom says after we've eaten. "You haven't told me how your tests went."

Mom sighs as she stretches out on our corduroy couch. I sit at the other end. When she puts her feet on my lap, I can't help feeling a little trapped.

I know Mom counts on my daily report. I also know I could never tell her about Mick. She wouldn't understand. She'd be like Polonius and try to talk me out of seeing him. Keeping secrets from her is a new feeling for me— one I'm not used to yet.

Mom wiggles her toes the way she does when she's happy. "Cal went fine," I tell her. "And I'm pretty sure I aced World History. Most people think World War I was caused by the assassination of Archduke Franz Ferdinand

and his wife, but there were other factors, like territorial disputes and the growth of nationalism across Europe." I don't know why I'm telling Mom all this. Maybe it's because I'm afraid I'll let something slip about Mick.

Mom doesn't seem to be suspicious. In fact, I think she's enjoying the world history lesson. "I've noticed that when things go wrong," she says. "There are usually lots of factors."

"Are you still working on that walk-in closet in the condo downtown?" I ask her.

Mom nods. "I'll be there for at least another week. That closet is bigger than your bedroom, Iris. The client wants a whole wall just for her shoes and boots. If you ask me, it's ridiculous. On the other hand, her shoe-and-boot habit pays our bills."

Mom wants to know if I have studying to do, and if I want to do it on the couch. "I could read my magazine," she says.

I lift her feet off my lap. "I need to start my English essay." Mom knows I prefer to write in my own room.

"You can read it to me when it's done."

Once I'm in my room, I let myself daydream about Mick. I see us walking along Mount Royal Avenue and sitting together in the café. I think about how much I want to kiss him.

I know I should start my essay before I get too tired.
Even if I only do the first couple of paragraphs. I will not
be the kind of girl who lets her schoolwork slide because
of some guy.

I flip open my laptop and create a new document. I write
my name and the course code at the top of the page.

Maybe I'll just take a short Facebook break. I check
the time at the top of the computer screen. I'm not going
to spend more than five minutes on Facebook, I promise
myself, then I'll go straight back to the essay.

I scan the latest postings. Antoine has posted a link to
a squirrel circus. A squirrel circus? No wonder Antoine's
failing chemistry. Katie's posted photos from today's
rehearsal. She must have shot them with her cell phone.
There's a photo of Tommy, adjusting a microphone. He's
wearing a *Star Wars* T-shirt that makes him look like he
did when we were in third grade—sweet and goofy. In the
background, I can just make out the tip of Mick's fedora.

I'm in the next photo. Mick is right—I do look better
with my hair off my face. My posture's better too. Even
though I've only known Mick for a short time, I know it's
because of him that I'm standing straighter.

Someone is sending me a personal message. I figure
it's Katie, asking for help with the English essay. But it isn't
her. The message is from someone named Nate Berg.

Oh my god. How weird is this?

Nate Berg is my father.

I nearly call out for my mom. She's still on the living-room couch, lost in the latest *Home Beautiful* magazine. But no, Mom would freak out.

My fingers tremble as I move the mouse to click on the message. Then I think, what if I don't open it? I've managed all these years without a father, thank you very much. Why do I need one now? I could delete the message without even looking at it. I could.

But I don't. I can hear my heart thumping under my T-shirt. I suck in my breath and click on the message.

My name is Nate Berg. I'm looking for the Iris Wagner who was born in Montreal on May 11, 1995. I'm her dad. Can you let me know if you are her? If you're not her, sorry to have bothered you.

It is him. My father. Nate Berg. I click on his name. There is no photo of him on his profile page. I check to see how many Facebook friends he has. None. That means Nate Berg opened a Facebook account to find me. But why now?

So much for my English essay.

I don't move. I just sit frozen in front of my computer screen, looking at Nate Berg's message, reading it over and over, as if it contains a secret meaning I might somehow have missed. *Can you let me know if you are her?*

I think about deleting the message. I could pretend I never got it. I could go on living my life the way I always have—without a father. But something stops me from deleting the message. Curiosity, I guess. What kind of a man is Nate Berg? Am I anything like him? And why has he waited so long to contact me?

I could answer the message right now and tell him that yes, it's me, Iris Wagner, and that's my birthdate. But I'm not sure I want to answer him, not sure I even want to be in touch. I've got to think about what to do. Besides, he's made me wait all these years. Now it's his turn to wait for me.

If only I could talk to Mom about what's happened, but I can't. She'd be upset. She'd get a headache or a stomachache; she might even cry. I can't put her through that. Not when she has sacrificed so much for me.

Even after I shut down the computer, I can still hear my father's words in my head, like a song you can't forget. Maybe I should write back to him. Maybe not. Maybe not yet. Maybe not ever.

It's late when I go to the kitchen to get a glass of water. My mom is still reading on the couch. "D'you want some water, Mom?"

"That would be nice, Iris."

She lays the magazine on her lap when I come into the living room. "How's the essay coming?"

43

"It's not going too well."

"You always say that when you're getting started on an essay."

"I do?"

Mom nods.

"Mom?"

"Yes, Iris."

I know I shouldn't mention my father, but I can't stop myself. "How come my father never tried to get in touch with me after he left the country?"

Mom sighs and looks down at the magazine on her lap. "Why are you asking me that now?"

She isn't going to answer my question, so I don't answer hers.

I go back upstairs with my glass of water. I'm shutting the door to my bedroom when I hear her calling out for me.

"Iris," she says, "sorry to be a nuisance. But could you get me an Advil from the bathroom cabinet?"

CHAPTER 7

"This is the very ecstasy of love..."
—*HAMLET*, ACT 2, SCENE 1

For the record: my life has officially begun.

I just had sex with Mick Horton, who is thirty-one and the hottest, sweetest guy ever. What's even more amazing is that Mick Horton had sex with *me*, Iris Wagner. Only I'm not the same Iris Wagner I was four hours ago. I'm new and totally one hundred percent improved. How couldn't I be? Of all the girls in Montreal, Mick Horton picked *me*. Mick Horton wants me. Really wants me.

We're stretched out on his bed now. Mick has dozed off, his back facing me. He has a great back, tanned and sinewy, with ripples of muscle in the right places. I'm lying on my side, admiring him and replaying every second of our night together.

We had dinner at this trendy sushi place on Saint Laurent Boulevard—the kind of place with dim lighting and beautiful waitresses in tight black dresses. Not that he was looking at them. I swear he never took his eyes off me. Mick makes me feel *seen*.

He ordered for both of us. We shared a platter with sashimi and California-style kamikaze rolls. Mick knows all about sushi. I swear he knows all about everything. We drank sake, which is hot wine that comes in a ceramic carafe.

I didn't get drunk or anything, just a bit buzzed. Besides, Mick didn't let me drink too much. He put his hand over my sake cup when the waiter wanted to refill it. I love how Mick wants to protect me.

He showed me how to use chopsticks. I'd tried using them before, but I'd always given up because it took too long. I loved the feeling of Mick's fingers pressing down on mine, showing me what to do.

We talked nonstop—about *Hamlet*, my career, even about my father. Mick thinks I need to answer the Facebook message. "Whatever happened between him and your mother is their business. You have your own relationship with him."

"But that's just it," I told Mick. "I've never had a relationship with him. Not one I can remember."

"Write back to him."

As soon as Mick said it, I knew it was the right thing to do.

"But what about my mom? Do you think I should tell her?"

Mick ran his finger back and forth over his soul patch. "From what you've told me, I'd say your mother doesn't want to know."

Afterward, Mick wanted me to see his loft. "We can work on your lines, Joey."

I laughed when he called me *Joey*.

"Are you calling me a baby kangaroo?"

Mick explained how Australians are big on nicknames.

I knew from the feeling I got when Mick put his hand on the small of my back and left it there that we weren't just going to his loft to work on my lines. I could've told him no. Part of me knew I shouldn't be going to see the loft of a guy I'd only just met, whose age I still didn't know and whom I couldn't tell anyone about. Not Katie, not my mom. But the sense that I was doing something wrong... well, it was another feeling I'm not used to, as if I were playing with fire—and it only made me want to do it more.

Mick has the coolest loft. It's in a high-rise on Cavendish Boulevard, where the street comes to an end. Mick says most of the other tenants in the building are seniors. Mick's renting a corner unit on the ninth floor. It's basically one room with high ceilings and giant floor-to-ceiling windows. When we looked out, we could see past Saint Joseph's Oratory to the lights on the top of Mount Royal.

The furniture's cool too, though Mick didn't pick it. Everything's chrome and glass—and there's a great black leather couch with zebra cushions.

In the end, I was glad I'd already had sex with Tommy. I didn't want Mick thinking I was just some kid.

We did work on my lines, like Mick said we would. He wanted to focus on Act II, Scene I. He said he'd read Polonius's part. "I'd never cast you as Polonius," I told him.

"I'll take that as a compliment."

"Polonius is a bore. You're...you're totally interesting."

"I've been accused of lots of things," Mick said. "Boring isn't one of them."

I closed my eyes as I prepared to become Ophelia. "'My lord,'" I whispered, "'as I was sewing in my closet...'"

That's when he kissed me. I knew it was coming, but that kiss still took me a little by surprise. For the tiniest second, I thought of backing away, of saying I shouldn't have come upstairs, but it was already too late for that. Besides, Mick's kiss was like no kiss I ever had before or ever even imagined. He slipped his hand behind my head (I could tell right away he knew exactly what he was doing) and brought my lips to his. The kiss started soft and gentle, but then it turned more...well, more urgent. Hungrier. A little rough, but not in a hurting way. More an exciting way. "Go on," Mick whispered. His voice was hoarse.

I knew what he wanted—for me to go on with my lines. "'As I was sewing in my closet, Lord Hamlet, with his doublet all unbraced...'"

That's when Mick unbuckled his jeans. His eyes were shining, playful. I felt like we were being childlike and grown up at the same time. "You mean *un*braced like this?" he asked, unzipping himself.

"Uh-huh." I was too excited to keep saying my lines.

"Or did you mean *em*braced—like this?"

He kissed me again. I could feel the stubble over his lips chafing my chin, my cheeks. Then he took off my clothes—and looked at me like I was the eighth wonder of the world. I'd have thought being naked like that would make me feel shy or embarrassed, but it didn't.

It was totally different than with Tommy. Tommy had been nervous and jumpy, like a puppy. Mick was more like a lynx, agile and in charge. He slid his hands all over me. Then he carried me from the leather couch to his bed. I couldn't have told him no even if I'd tried to.

Mick said he loves everything about me. My face, my body, my hair (now that I wear it off my face), even the way I sometimes cackle when I laugh.

"Joey, touch some part of me that begins with an...*h*."

I touched his head.

"Your turn," he said.

"I like this game. Touch some part of me that begins with an…*e*."

Mick touched my eyelid. No one's ever touched my eyelid before.

We went through practically the whole alphabet. We got stuck on *x* and *z* and *q*.

Maybe I should've waited to have sex with Mick till I knew him better. Katie says there's a five-date rule, that you need to go out with a guy five times before you do it. And two dates on the same day don't count. But Katie's never been with Mick.

The thing is, I feel like I've known Mick forever. More dates wouldn't have made a difference.

The other thing is, I can't resist him.

CHAPTER 8

"...there is nothing either good or bad,
but thinking makes it so." —HAMLET, ACT 2, SCENE 2

It's Sunday, and I just got home from Scoops. I need to shower to get rid of the ice-cream smell inside my nose. My back and feet feel sore, but part of me is still floating from having spent the first part of the weekend with Mick. *Mick!* It's not the first time I catch myself saying his name out loud—the way Ophelia does when she thinks of Hamlet.

In the shower, I watch the water stream down my body—over all the places Mick touched.

Afterward, I go to my room and shut the door behind me. I take a deep breath before I start typing.

My name is Iris Wagner and I was born on May 11, 1995.

I nearly send just that as my reply to my father, but then I decide I have some questions of my own. So I add another sentence. My fingers tremble as I type.

Where are you and why are you getting in touch with me now?

I can feel my heart pumping underneath my T-shirt.

Nate Berg's reply pops up almost immediately. What's he been doing—waiting by the computer since he first wrote to me?

I am in Bangkok. I've tried to get in touch before, but your mother blocked my attempts. A friend here suggested I look for you on Facebook.

Mom blocked his attempts? That can't be true. Why would Mom do something like that?

Well, now you've found me.

My heart is still pumping hard. I want to shut down Facebook. But there is already another message from Nate Berg. I can't call him my dad. I know the mailman better than I know him.

I want to see you, Iris.

See me?

I get up from my desk. I stretch my arms over my head. From my bedroom window, I can see a man and his son walking a small dog. The boy runs ahead and his father calls him back. I peer out at the street. When I turn around, the computer screen is glowing in the dark room. I try to imagine my father, sitting in a small room somewhere in Bangkok, waiting for my answer.

I heard you weren't allowed into the country.

There, I think. I'm glad I said it. Let him know I'm on to him. That I know he did something illegal.

You're right. I can't come to Canada. But I have busi-ness in the US next month. We could meet in Plattsburgh, New York. It's only an hour's drive from Montreal. What do you say, Iris?

What do I say?

I have no friggin' idea what I say.

I need Mick to help me figure things out. I can't talk to him at school—not with everyone around—so I phone him on Monday night. Just hearing his voice makes me feel calmer. "I can only tell you one thing, Joey," Mick says. "I wish I'd been able to set things right with my own dad. This is your chance. If you do decide to meet him in Plattsburgh, I could drive you there. We could make a day of it."

"You'd do that for me?"

"What wouldn't I do for you?"

~

The following Saturday, I'm awake before Mick. For a while, I just lie there, admiring him and feeling grateful that this is my life. Mick looks so peaceful when he's sleeping, the dark hairs on his chest rising and falling with every breath. I snuggle closer. Mick smells so good, so warm.

When I'm too awake to stay in bed, I get up and turn on my laptop. My father and I have messaged each other a few more times since I talked things through with Mick. I said I'd meet him in Plattsburgh—and I asked him to send me his photo. So I'd recognize him.

This morning, the photo is there.

Everyone always says how much I look like my mom. I have her wavy auburn hair and green eyes, and we're both slim and on the short side. But now, when I look at the photo of my dad, I see myself too. I recognize the high cheekbones, the way his eyes seem wider apart than most people's. I wonder if when my mom looks at me, she sees him too, and I wonder how that makes her feel.

Mick startles me when he kisses my shoulder. I didn't realize he was standing behind me. "Is that him?" he asks. "Daddy-o?"

"Uh-huh. It's him. What do you think?"

"It's hard to tell much from a photo. Not a bad-looking guy. Did you tell him I'd be coming with you to Plattsburgh?"

"I told him. And I explained you were just a friend." I watch Mick's face when I tell him that. I know he'll be pleased.

Mick nods. "That's my Joey."

"He needed to know your name."

Mick has stretched out on the floor to do his morning push-ups. "My name?" he says, without looking up from the floor. "What for?"

"He says my passport might not be enough. He's going to fax us a letter saying he's authorized you to take me over the border. To see him. Because I'm still a minor." I whisper that last part. I don't want to remind Mick of our age difference.

I hope Mick won't be upset that I've given his name to my father. But Mick doesn't seem to mind. He's finished his push-ups and is stretching out his calves. "It's probably a good idea," he says, stroking his soul patch. "I gather he knows a thing or two about rules and regulations."

I don't mention Katie's birthday party until Mick's had his tea. He doesn't want me to go. "Just tell her you're too busy. Tell her you're working on your lines tonight."

Mick is making French toast, sprinkling it with icing sugar.

My cell phone rings. The call display says *Mom*. "I'd better get it," I tell Mick.

"Hi, Mom," I say. Then I yawn into the phone. "What's up?" I can't help assessing my own performance. Convincing. A seventeen-year-old girl just waking up on a Saturday morning at her best friend's house.

I put my hand over the phone so Mick won't hear her asking if I remembered to floss last night. "Why are you whispering?" she asks.

"Katie's parents are sleeping in." I'm surprised at how easily the lie comes to me. I'm getting used to lying to my mom. It's another way my life has changed since I met Mick. "Love you, Mom." That part, at least, is true.

Mom sighs on the other end of the phone. "Love you, dolly." I hope Mick didn't hear that.

I've been at Mick's a lot in the last two weeks. The fact that we get along so well in such a small place proves how amazing we are together. We haven't had a single fight. And I'm not going to fight about Katie's birthday.

Still, I feel guilty about missing it. "I haven't missed one of Katie's parties in ten years! I hate to let her down." I make a pouty face, which works when I want something from my mom, but it doesn't work on Mick.

"Stop pouting," he tells me, and his tone is firmer than I'm used to. "Don't you see, Joey? You've outgrown Katie. You're going to need to let some things—and some people—go if you want to keep moving forward in your life. You want to move forward, don't you, Joey?" Mick moves in close when he asks me that. His dark eyes lock on mine. Mick says life is all about moving forward.

"Of course, I do. It's just…"

"Just what?" I hate that he sounds impatient. I want the gentle Mick back.

"Just nothing." I cut my French toast into perfect squares. For the first time since we've been together, I don't know if I can tell Mick what I'm thinking. What I'm really hoping for. I know he's got lots on his mind. He's been on the phone nonstop with his lawyer in Melbourne; they're trying to reach a settlement with Nial's mom about child support. Mick also has to decide whether to take a directing gig here in Montreal. "The work's not nearly as prestigious as the stuff I've been doing in Australia," he explained to me last night. "I need to think about what's best for my career, but let's just say Montreal has its perks." When he said that, he reached under my T-shirt and into my bra and tweaked my nipple. He tweaked a little too hard, and when I put on my bra this morning, my nipple still felt tender.

I haven't told anyone about Mick and me. There've been a couple of times when I wanted to tell Katie— mainly so she wouldn't keep thinking I was such an innocent. But there are people who know—or who must be figuring it out. Like Mrs. Karpman, the elderly woman who lives in the apartment next to Mick's loft. She has a pet canary. I know because I hear it chirping when she lets herself in. "Nice to see you again, dear," she said when we bumped into each other in the hallway yesterday.

Her voice is low and raspy, and there's a scar on her throat. She must have had some kind of throat surgery. Her hearing is bad too, because she wears hearing aids in both ears, and when I speak, I see she's watching my lips.

"Mick…" I reach out across the narrow table for Mick's hand. This isn't easy for me, but I need to be able to tell Mick how I feel and what I want. "Would you come with me to Katie's party?" I ask in a small voice. "Please." No pouting this time.

Mick gets up from the stool he's been sitting on. The more time we spend together, the better I'm getting at reading his moods. It's another sign of how close we are. Now I can see the weather on his face has changed, gone stormy. "Iris!" he says so loudly that even if Mrs. Karpman hasn't put in her hearing aids she will hear him, "what's wrong with you?"

I don't know what to answer when he asks me that. "There's nothing wrong with me," I start to tell him—but as soon as I say it, I know it's not true. It was stupid of me to ask him to come. I know how important it is to Mick that we keep our relationship a secret. "It's just…just… well…Katie's been my best friend since second grade. Couldn't we just drop by? We could say we ran into each other on the str—"

"No!" Mick's eyes are flashing in a way I'm not used to. In a way that makes me nervous. Instead of being quiet, which would probably be smarter right now, I keep talking. I can't help it. "I mean…we are together…aren't we?"

I don't know why Mick is getting so angry. I reach for his shoulder, thinking that will calm him down, but it doesn't. It makes things worse. Mick shrugs me away. For some reason, I notice his nostrils. They are flaring like a horse's. Then, out of nowhere, Mick extends his forearm and punches the wall between the kitchen nook and the window.

I shudder. If I'd been standing just a few inches closer, he'd have hit me.

"Mick! Stop it!" I'm shouting now too and crying at the same time. I'm too upset to think about Mrs. Karpman.

Mick's hand is swelling up. The poor guy! What if he's fractured a knuckle or his wrist? I need to get him some ice right away.

There is an ugly fist-size hole in the plaster. I close my eyes so I won't have to see it.

Mick's cell phone rings. "Damn it to hell," he mutters. I rush to the kitchen for the ice. Mick is checking the caller ID on his phone. "It's the lawyer again," he says. "I need to take this."

His voice is totally normal when he answers the call. How can he turn his emotions on and off like that? "Chuck," he says evenly. "Give me a minute. I want to take this call outside."

I stuff the ice cubes into a plastic bag. Mick grabs the bag from me without a word and walks out the door.

The loft feels eerie without Mick. I throw out my French toast. I'm not hungry anymore.

I remember seeing a hammer in one of the drawers in the kitchen. There are two framed prints on the wall behind the sofa. One's a line drawing of the Bonsecours Market in Old Montreal. The other is more abstract— bright orange lines intersecting with pale blue ones. I'll take the one of the Bonsecours Market and hang it over the hole Mick's fist left in the plaster. Then we can pretend this never happened.

CHAPTER 9

"Beware of entrance to a quarrel..."
—*HAMLET*, ACT 1, SCENE 3

When I go home the next morning, I'm surprised to find Mom sitting on our living-room couch, wearing her velour housecoat and sipping green tea. Lately, the Clear Your Clutter Closet Company has been so busy that Mom has been working weekends too. She isn't good at turning down jobs. Maybe it's because, from what I understand, we were seriously broke after she and my dad split up. It took her years to pay off the debts he'd left, and I guess she got into the habit of working hard. I worry about Mom getting run-down. But there's a plus side too: she works so much she hasn't noticed how little time I'm actually spending at home.

"Hey, you're home." I hand Mom the newspaper, which I've brought in from the porch.

Mom removes the thick elastic band that's keeping the newspaper rolled up and pops the blue band into the cup she uses for collecting elastics. Then she taps her cheek. It's something she's done since I was little—her signal that she wants a kiss.

Even though I'm not five anymore, I kiss her. For the first time, I see myself playing the role of devoted daughter. Which feels a little confusing. I've always been devoted to my mom. But things feel different—I feel different—since I started lying to her and since I've been in contact with my father.

Mom's face smells lotiony. There are new lines over her lips and by her eyes. "I had a last-minute cancellation," she tells me. "One of my clients' cars needs a new transmission. They're going to hold off on redesigning their closets till next fall. To be honest, I'm great with it. I need some downtime. And this way we can spend the day together, Iris. How 'bout breakfast at our bagel place? And a DVD tonight? Like old times." She must catch me biting my lip because she adds, "Unless you've got other plans, sweetpie."

I could object to being called *sweetpie*, but I don't. "I can do breakfast, but then I need to get back to"—I pause to give myself time to get my story straight—"to school. For rehearsal. And I promised Katie I'd sleep over tonight."

"But you slept there last night." Mom's voice is neutral. Not hurt. Definitely not suspicious. Even so, I can't help feeling guilty.

"Things get kind of intense, Mom, when you're in rehearsal."

"I know they do. And I respect that you work so hard. Really I do. But you do seem to be doing an awful lot of rehearsing for a high school production..." Mom lets her voice trail off. She knows this is a sensitive subject for me.

"It's more than a high school production, Mom. Ms. Cameron says she's making a point of treating us like professionals. So we can get a feeling for what acting is really all about."

"All right, Iris. I respect that. I think it's great that you're learning so much from Ms. Cameron. Hey, before I forget to ask—how was Katie's birthday bash?"

When I hear the word *bash*, I can't help picturing the hole Mick made in the wall. I try to push the thought as far away as I can. I don't want Mom to see it on my face. "Amazing." Short answers make lying easier.

"D'you want to have some green tea or should we head right out for those bagels?"

"We should probably get there before the line gets too long."

Mom tightens her housecoat around her waist as she gets up from the couch. Then she runs her hand over my forehead. "You're gorgeous, Iris, but I have to tell you—you look a little stressed. Maybe it's all that rehearsing."

There's already a lineup when we get to the bagel place, but because there are only two of us, we don't have to wait very long. A woman sitting by the brick wall waves. Mom did her closets two years ago. "Hoarder," Mom says under her breath. "One of the worst cases I've ever seen. She's got ten years of newspapers piled up in her hallway. You have to walk sideways to get to her kitchen."

I peek over my shoulder at the woman. Her hair is stylishly cut and she's laughing at something her friend just said. I'd never have guessed she's a hoarder, which goes to show how little you can tell from looking at a person.

"Do people ever ask you to sign a confidentiality agreement?" I ask Mom when we're seated across from each other. "Like a lawyer or an accountant?"

Mom's laugh has a tinkling sound. When I was little, her laugh made me laugh, but now I look around at the nearby tables, hoping the people sitting at them are too busy eating to notice it. "It'd probably be a good idea for some of my customers," Mom says. "But it'd be awful for me. I'd have nothing to talk about. Except you, of course." Mom takes my hand and squeezes it. I want her to let go—it's embarrassing to be seventeen and holding hands with your mother in public—but I know if I shake my hand loose, it'll hurt her feelings.

Thank God Mom releases my hand when the waitress comes over. I make a point of asking the waitress how she's doing. I also take the napkins and cutlery she's carrying and put everything in the right spot. I know how tough it is to stay on top of things when a restaurant gets busy.

"Thanks," the waitress says. Our eyes meet for a moment, and I know she knows I'm a waitress too. It's like being part of a secret society. Freemasons have a secret handshake; waitresses help each other with cutlery.

Mom points to the bottom of her menu. "We'll have our usual. Scrambled eggs with sesame-seed bagels. Toasted. Fruit salad instead of home fries. Please." Mom hands the menu back to the waitress.

My hands are in my lap now—safely out of Mom's reach.

"I'll have poached eggs, not scrambled, please," I tell the waitress.

"Sure," she says, scratching something out on her pad.

"Sweetpie!" Mom says. (The waitress gives me a sympathetic look.) "Poached eggs? Since when do you like poached eggs?"

"I guess I'm in the mood for a change. Besides, I'm starting to like poached eggs. I've been eating them at"—lying is harder than acting because you have to make up the script as you go along—"Katie's."

Mom's not good with change, even if it involves eggs. I think if she had her way, she'd keep me a little girl forever. Not because she doesn't want me to grow up and have my own life; I think Mom just got used to having a little girl around for company.

"Iris," she says, "why don't we plan to come here for breakfast every single weekend? If we did it first thing on Saturdays, I could still—"

"Mom." My voice comes out sharper than I want it to. "I can't go making plans like that. Not with the play coming up."

This time, Mom bites her lip. "You're right. I'm being a pest. So tell me *everything*..."

I have a sudden urge to check the time on my cell phone. I'm meeting Mick back at the loft at one.

There's no way I'm going to tell my mom *everything*, but I know I've got to tell her *something*.

"I'm really getting into Ophelia's character."

"That's wonderful," Mom says.

I'm waiting for her to say what she usually does—that I should probably have a Plan B—but she doesn't. That makes me want to tell her a little more.

"Ophelia is really close with her brother and her dad. So she's super torn when her dad says he thinks Hamlet's totally wrong for her. But the thing is, Ophelia's crazy in love with Hamlet." Just saying the words *crazy in love* makes me think of Mick and how I'm crazy in love with him. His lips, his shoulders, the way he calls me *Joey* and holds me so tight it almost hurts to breathe.

"It's been ages since I read the play, but wasn't Hamlet bonkers?" Mom asks, twirling one finger in a circle by the side of her head to emphasize *bonkers*.

"He's brilliant, not bonkers. And it doesn't hurt that he's a prince."

"A difficult prince," Mom says. "Why is it some women always fall for difficult guys?"

I want to ask Mom whether my father was difficult. But I can't. My father has always been the forbidden topic in our lives. Besides, I already know he was difficult. That's why they broke up and also why I'm supposed to be grateful he didn't make an effort to stay in touch with me. Only maybe what he wrote to me is true—maybe he did make an effort. Maybe Mom blocked it. But why?

Take it from me—we're better off without him. Mom said that so many times when I was little, I took it for a fact. Now I'm not so sure.

The waitress brings our food. Mom gives me a suspicious look as I break off a piece of toasted bagel and dip it in the runny egg yolks.

"Speaking of princes," she says, "how're you and Tommy managing? He really is a lovely guy. So respectful. Not at all bonkers, like that Hamlet of yours. I'm really glad you chose someone who's good for you. Some women have such awful taste in men." I wonder if she's talking about herself. Does Mom worry that bad taste in men is a genetic trait I might have inherited—like green eyes or wavy hair?

I hate disappointing Mom, but I don't want her holding out hope for me and Tommy. "I'm not really with Tommy anymore." I'm playing with my napkin, folding it into smaller and smaller triangles.

"I had no idea." This time, Mom does sound hurt. You'd think she was the one who'd just gone through a breakup. "How come?" She leans in a little closer, and I know that if my hand was on the table, she'd be squeezing it. I know Mom wants me to tell her *everything*—the way I used to when I was little. And part of me wants to because it felt good to tell someone everything—to let out whatever was going on in my heart and head. But I know I can't. Not just because things are too complicated right now, but because I'm not Mom's little girl anymore. No matter how much she wants me to be.

CHAPTER 10

"Doubt truth to be a liar,
But never doubt I love." —*HAMLET*, ACT 2, SCENE 2

I take off my jean jacket and sling it over my arm. The weather's so mild, it feels more like May than October. I heard on the radio that Indian summer is coming later than it used to. Scientists think it could be another sign of global warming. I wish I could just enjoy the warm air, but I worry about the planet. How will global warming affect my kids? Our kids? I'd never tell Mick, but sometimes I let myself daydream about the children we'll have one day. I know they'll be into acting. I hope they have my green eyes—and Mick's confidence.

There's no answer when I buzz the loft. I'm buzzing a second time when Mrs. Karpman—Mick's neighbor— opens the glass door in the lobby for me. Her eyeglasses are dangling from the end of a long sparkly chain hanging around her neck. With every breath, her scar pulses.

"I have something for you, dear," she says, handing me an envelope. "It's from your friend upstairs."

"Thanks," I say as I tear the envelope open. Why in the world would Mick write me a letter? And then a dark cloud crosses my mind. What if he's going back to Melbourne? What if he's already left? The idea of having to live without him makes my arms go limp. But no, he'd never take off without telling me. Never. Katie thinks I've got abandonment issues on account of my dad's having left when I was so little. I remind myself now that Mick is nothing like my dad. Mick would never abandon me.

"What does it say?" a small raspy voice is asking. I've forgotten Mrs. Karpman, who is still standing by the glass door, propping it open with her crocheted purse.

Mick has written to me on a sheet of thick cream-colored stationery. I even love his handwriting—its boldness, the forceful strokes across his *Ts*. The letter is only two sentences long, but they take up the whole page: *There's a Diamond taxi waiting outside the apartment building. Get in it. Your Mick.*

I don't even realize I am reading the letter out loud.

My heart swells in my chest at the *Your Mick* part. *My Mick.* I love the sound of that. Who cares that Mick doesn't say please—or that the message sounds bossy? *Get in it.* Mick's not bossy. He's old-fashioned and romantic. He likes to take charge, and I like how that feels.

How could I have worried? Am I that insecure? Mick would never go back to Australia without me!

Katie says that in every couple, there's always someone who loves the other person more—but that isn't true with Mick and me. No way. He loves me just as much as I love him. Loving Mick—and being loved by him—makes me feel like the luckiest girl in all the world, ever. Other guys might be handsome or fun or talented or have a great sense of humor or be smart and sophisticated, but Mick's all those things. So what if he's fourteen years older than me? I could never be with a boy my own age. I could never talk to some seventeen-year-old boy the way I can talk to Mick.

Mrs. Karpman is beaming up at me. "That Aussie of yours is quite a charmer." She says the word *charmer* in a neutral way, as if she isn't quite sure it's a good thing. "All he would tell me is he's planned a surprise for you. I must admit, it makes me miss my Nelson. Not that he was one for surprises. Still, once you get to my age, it's nice to be part of someone's surprise. I just hope he's kind to you, dear."

"Of course he's kind to me. I've never known anyone kinder." And because I'm so happy and excited and relieved that Mick hasn't run off without telling me, I hug Mrs. Karpman, hard.

Even her laughter comes out raspy. "Drop by and see me sometime," she says, her voice sounding even more strained from all the excitement. "I want you to meet Sunshine, my canary. He'd enjoy the company."

Just as Mick said, there's a Diamond taxi waiting outside. "You Iris?" the cabbie asks, turning to look at me when I get in.

I'm too excited to do anything but nod—and smile so hard my cheeks ache. When I look at my reflection in the rearview mirror, I decide I have never seen myself look so totally, completely happy. Maybe Mick's right. Maybe I am beautiful. There is something different about my eyes. I think it's that I look happier and more confident. It's hard to remember who I was before I met Mick. I was a plant withering on a shady windowsill. Mick is water and sun to me. He's made me come alive in a way I never had before.

The cab is heading east along Côte-St-Luc Road toward downtown. "Where are you taking me exactly?" I ask the cabbie, trying not to giggle. Though it shouldn't matter what he thinks of me, I don't want him to think I'm some silly teenager.

The cabbie meets my eyes in the rearview mirror. "I'm not supposed to say."

I feel like a star. If only I could text or phone someone to say how happy I am and how amazingly wonderful and totally perfect Mick is. That's the thing about good news—a person can't help wanting to share it. Bad news is different—at least for me. When there's bad news, I just want to make it go away. Of course, I can't tell anyone my good news. No one is supposed to know about Mick and me. Unless you count Mrs. Karpman.

The cabbie pulls up in front of an expensive flower shop, the kind that sells tall bouquets of exotic feathery flowers. "You're supposed to go inside there," the cabbie says. "Then we go to your next stop."

There's a man in a white apron by the refrigerator. He's holding a bouquet wrapped in thick cellophane. "Love your name," he says when he spots me—and that's when I realize he's holding a bouquet of irises! Pale mauve with slivers of yellow. I take the bouquet and press my nose against a little opening in the plastic wrap. The irises smell like...like...grape bubblegum. I take another sniff.

I can't believe Mick has done all this for me! Me!

Our next stop is a French patisserie on Côte-des-Neiges Road.

What am I supposed to do now? Go to the counter and ask if there's a box of pastries with my name on it? Just as I'm trying to figure out my next move, my eyes land on a wall with a bulletin board. The bulletin board is crammed with ads for concerts and lectures. A string quartet, chamber music, a lecture about grief and another about using tough love on your kids. And now, beside all the ads, I see a photo of Mick that's been made into a black-and-white poster. I laugh out loud when I see it.

I can't believe the trouble Mick has gone to, all for me! So what if he won't let me tell anyone about us? This treasure hunt—because now I realize that is what this is—proves Mick loves me as much as I love him. Maybe even more. The thought makes me feel more drunk than when I had that cup of sake on our first date.

The photo must be an old PR shot because Mick looks younger than he is now. For a second, I'm wistful. If only the me I am now had known him then—we'd be closer in age and we wouldn't have to keep our relationship a secret. Of course, that makes no sense. I was probably ten when Mick posed for that photo.

On the poster there's a note I know is meant for me. Mick must have come here himself this morning to hang it up. The note tells me to look underneath the small round table at the back of the patisserie. I practically dance over to the table.

I find a large cardboard box with another pale mauve iris fastened to it. Little tears sting the corners of my eyes. So this, I think, is what it feels like to cry from happiness.

When my cell phone rings and I answer, it feels like I'm onstage. Only I'm not Ophelia pining for Hamlet. I'm the lead in a play an internationally acclaimed director has created just for me, Iris Wagner.

I put my bouquet and my box down on the table.

Mick's voice is warm caramel. "Go to the curb outside. And close your eyes."

I do exactly what he says. I like when Mick directs me.

Even with my eyes closed, I can feel him. First he takes the box and the bouquet from my hands, then he takes me in his arms and spins me round and round, faster and faster. Part of me feels all grown up; another part feels like a little girl. A very happy little girl. A happier little girl than I ever was when I was little.

"Keep your eyes closed, Joey," his warm-caramel voice whispers in my ear.

Mick leads me back to the cab, and we sit in the backseat, our thighs pressed together. "No, no," Mick says when I try to open my eyes. He slips his hand under my skirt and runs his fingers along the inside of my leg. I hope the cabbie isn't watching now. I try pushing Mick's hand away, but he won't let me. He presses his fingertips into my skin.

When the cab drives up a hill, I know we must be headed for Mount Royal. Mick insists I keep my eyes closed when he helps me out of the car and afterwards, when we are walking through a park. I have to hold on to his arm so I don't fall.

"All right, you can open your eyes now, Joey."

We are standing at the edge of Beaver Lake. It's like being in a postcard. The trees in the distance are so orange and red, they look like they're on fire. The water in front of us is dark and has a delicious briny smell. A family of ducks is swimming in our direction. Has Mick arranged this too?

The ducks quack expectantly. Mick opens the cardboard box from the patisserie and takes out a bag of cubed baguette. He's thought of everything—even feeding the ducks. "You give it to them, Joey," he says.

I feel Mick watching me, and I know that making me happy makes him happy. Which makes me even happier. More than anything else, I want to make Mick happy too. I'd do anything to make him happy. I know his life isn't easy—he has work demands, and then there's all the trouble he still has to sort out with his ex-wife—but I know if I love him right, I can make things easier for him. This is what love is. Putting the person you love before yourself. Sometimes even forgetting yourself because the other person's happiness matters so much to you.

I'm guessing we're going to have a picnic here at the park. We're not the only ones taking advantage of this warm October day. Other couples have already staked out spots under the giant maples; families with small children are fanned out closer to the playground.

But leave it to Mick. He's planned another sort of picnic. One I'll bet nobody else ever thought of.

He's rented a yellow plastic pedal boat for the afternoon. We pedal out to the middle of the lake, and again, he makes me shut my eyes.

"Okay, you can look now."

"Mick!" Mick has laid out a small red-and-white-checked cloth across the plastic divider between our seats. There's a sandwich for each of us and a tub of couscous salad with fat golden raisins. I hear a popping sound, and I see that Mick has even brought along a mini bottle of champagne and two collapsible plastic wine goblets. He pours a glass of champagne for me, then one for him.

"What are we toasting?"

"Let's toast to now," Mick says. "Life is about now." The words are simple, but coming from Mick, they sound deep. He's right, of course. That's all life is—now—and we need to celebrate it. Mick is teaching me that.

"To now!" I know it's real champagne because Katie told me real champagne isn't too sweet the way fake champagne is. Even a small bottle must have cost a lot.

Mick even loosens the plastic wrapping around the irises and hangs the bouquet from the side of the pedal boat so the ends of the stems will stay moist.

A woman is pointing at us from the path at the edge of the lake. She must be noticing the irises and our picnic stuff. I'll bet she wishes she had a boyfriend who was as romantic as Mick. A teenage boy has come to stand next to the woman. It has to be Antoine—no one else I've ever met has hair as big and frizzy as his.

I don't tell Mick about Antoine. Instead, I point toward the other end of the lake. "See that hill over there? That's where we go tobogganing in winter."

Mick and I pedal in that direction. Our feet move in perfect synchronization.

When we are both out of breath, we stop to take a break. Antoine—and his hair—are out of sight.

"I have one more surprise for you, Joey," Mick says, reaching into his pocket and pulling out another sheet of cream-colored stationery. This one is folded into a square. Mick hands it to me and I unfold it.

"You wrote me a poem?"

"What can I say?" Mick shrugs his shoulders. "You inspire me."

When I read the poem Mick has written for me, I forget all about the ducks, Beaver Lake, the couscous salad and the real champagne.

"*Until you.*" I read that first line out loud, but when I get to the second line, my voice cracks.

"*I was small and lost, like a rudderless ship.*"

I read the rest of the poem to myself. It's not easy, because my eyes are tearing up again and I have to keep wiping them.

Until you.
Nothing made sense.
Not a thing.
Not power, not work.
Not fame or success.
Until you.
I couldn't feel, not really feel.
Body or soul,
Until you were mine.
Mine to hold,
To shape
Like sweet soft clay.
I love you
So much I can't say.
So much
It hurts.

CHAPTER 11

"Mark the encounter."
—HAMLET, ACT 2, SCENE 2

"What's your relationship?" The customs inspector peers into the Jeep. I can see him taking it all in—Mick, who has removed his sunglasses, in the driver's seat; me sitting next to him, my legs neatly crossed; the plastic water bottles at my feet; the pile of scripts in the backseat.

"We're together," I answer.

"We're friends," Mick says over me.

"Passports, please." The inspector flips through Mick's passport first, pausing to look at some of the stamps inside. Mick has traveled to so many places. "So you're Australian?"

"Yes, sir." Though the inspector is younger than Mick, Mick is being extremely polite.

"Ever seen a kangaroo?" the inspector asks.

"Lots of times," Mick says.

The inspector opens my passport. "Where are you two heading today?"

"To Plattsburgh," I answer. "We're going to meet up with my fa—"

Mick takes over. "With her father. He lives in Bangkok, but he's in the US on business. We have this letter from him." Mick reaches between the two seats for the letter my father has faxed. "It authorizes me to accompany Iris to Plattsburgh."

The inspector unfolds the letter. He looks up at me as he reads it, then nods. "How long will you be in the United States?"

Mick eyes the clock on the dashboard. "About six hours in total. I'll drop Iris back at her house tonight." It's a lie, of course. Mick obviously doesn't want the border inspector to know I'll be spending the night with Mick like I do every Saturday night.

The inspector taps something into his computer, then waves us through. Mick puts his sunglasses back on and checks his reflection in the rearview mirror. "Next time," he says without looking at me, "let me do the talking, all right?"

If Mick notices I'm quieter than usual, he doesn't mention it. He knows I'm nervous. I glance at the clock. We're meeting my father at a restaurant called Friendly's in downtown Plattsburgh.

We can see the red and white sign almost as soon as we exit the highway. Mick reaches out to squeeze my hand. "I'll be right beside you, Joey."

What do you say to a father you haven't seen in over twelve years—and whom you can't remember? Why didn't I think to come up with a list of things to talk about?

I recognize him right away. He is sitting in a booth at the front of the restaurant, watching for me.

He knows it's me too. He stands up (he's taller than I expected), and for a second I worry that he is going to try and hug me, but he reaches for my hand instead.

"I-ris." He says my name slowly, like he's been practicing it for a long time. He has a goofy, lopsided smile. The kind of smile that must make people like him. But I won't let him win me over with that smile—not just like that. Not after what he's done to my mom—and to me.

"Mick, right?" He shakes Mick's hand. "Iris's friend?" Is it my imagination or does he sound suspicious? "Thanks so much for giving her a ride today. Everything go okay at the border?"

I slide into the booth, across from my father. Mick sits next to me, but he leaves enough room between us for a whole other person. I'd feel better if he was sitting closer to me.

My father beams at me. "I can't tell you how happy I am that you're here, Iris. That we're together. And I have to say—you're lovely. Really, really lovely."

"Thanks." I feel myself smiling back, even if I don't want to.

"You have your mother's eyes. She had the most amazing eyes." He leans in closer, resting his elbows on the table. "To be honest, Iris, I worried...well...that you might not even open that message I sent." He watches my face as he speaks, as if he's gauging how much he can say.

"I almost didn't open it."

He nods to let me know he understands. "I'm glad you did. So glad." He clears his throat. "Well then, we've got some important decisions to make."

Mick looks up from his menu. I know he's been listening to every word, watching out for me. If there are important decisions to make, Mick will want to be involved.

But then my father grins and waves the menu. "I'm dying for pancakes. What about you two?"

I can't help laughing. Mick laughs too. It's getting harder to resist my father's smile.

We all order pancakes. "Pancakes were one of the first things you ever ate," my father tells me. "Only I think you liked the maple syrup more than the pancakes. You got your sweet tooth from me." He taps his chest, then looks at me. "This feels pretty weird, doesn't it?"

"That's for sure," I tell him.

"Well, we've got to start somewhere," he says. "Today's our start."

I nearly tell him our start was seventeen years ago.

"I still can't get over what a beauty you are. Not that you weren't a beauty when you were little. I'm the one who picked your name. Did you know that?"

"No."

My father closes his eyes. It gives me a chance to study his face. There are bags under his eyes and the skin on his cheeks is slack, but he is still a handsome man. He would have been even handsomer when Mom fell in love with him. He opens his eyes. "Your mom and I had a patch of purple irises in the backyard. And a little yellow birdhouse on our elm tree. You used to love to sit by the window in your high chair and watch the birds fly in and out."

"I did?"

"I remember it like it was yesterday."

I don't have the heart to tell him I don't remember any of it. That I hardly remember him.

I know it's silly, but I'm bothered when my father turns to Mick. Katie might be right: maybe I do have abandonment issues. "So how do you know Iris exactly?"

"We've been working together on a theater production. Iris is very talented."

"Of course she is," my father says.

He turns back to me. "You said you're playing Ophelia. How's that going for you? You getting into character? Making the transition from obedient daughter to desperate lovelorn girlfriend?"

I didn't expect him to use an acting expression like *getting into character* or for him to know so much about Ophelia. "It's going pretty well. I really like being her. I like how she feels things so deeply. I can relate to that."

My father nods. His eyes sparkle in a way that makes him look even more handsome. "I know exactly what you mean about relating. I guess you know I did a little acting at university...before..."

For a moment, I wonder if I've heard right. "You were an actor?"

My father laughs. The laugh, low at first but building almost to a cackle, startles me. It sounds so much like mine. "I wouldn't call myself an actor. But I was in a couple of shows when your mom and I were at McGill. I figured she'd have mentioned—"

"She doesn't like to talk about you. It upsets her."

My father runs one of his fingers over his lips, then crosses his hands on the table. "I can't say I blame her. I put her through the ringer..." He sighs, as if he regrets all the trouble he caused. "After everything happened"—he doesn't say what *everything* is—"and I had to leave the country, I tried to talk her into coming with me. So the three of us could be together." It's not hard to tell he still feels sorry for himself. As if he thinks he's the one who suffered most.

"You abandoned me," I tell him. "You abandoned us."

He winces. "I guess it looks that way, doesn't it? But Iris, I need you to know I wish things could've been different." He looks down at his plate and then back up at me. "A girl needs a father," he says softly.

"I've done okay without you."

"I can see that. I'm proud of you, Iris. Really, I am." His eyes are getting misty. I can tell he's trying to swallow back his tears—the way I am. I don't want to feel sorry for him, but it's hard not to.

"I don't need you to be proud of me. I don't need you at all." Somehow, I manage to say it without crying.

My father wipes his eyes with his napkin.

I feel Mick's palm on my knee now, steadying me. I take a deep breath.

What would my life have been like, I wonder, if Mom and I had followed this man? I'd have grown up somewhere else. And I'd probably never have met Mick.

My father clears his throat. "Look, I don't want to badmouth your mother—"

"Then don't."

"Well, let's say she can be pretty tough. She insisted on full custody. She knew I wouldn't fight her. Couldn't fight her. I had my hands full"—he looks down at his hands—

"with business matters. I tried to stay in touch, Iris. You've got to believe me. I used to phone. But she didn't want me talking to you. Then she changed the number. It killed me."

"You're still here."

"You know what I mean."

Thank God for Mick. I could never handle this alone. Having Mick here makes me feel stronger.

The waitress brings our food, and Mick waits until we are eating our pancakes before he speaks. He must sense that my conversation with my father has gone far enough. "So what kind of work are you doing in Bangkok?" Mick's voice is calm, interested.

"I'm an...an investor. In telecommunications. We're working on some new products. They're going to revolutionize the industry." My father's voice sounds lighter, brighter, comfortable. As if he's said these same things many times before.

"That sounds promising," Mick says. I can't tell if he means it.

My father checks his cell phone, which he's left out on the table, near his napkin. He sees that I notice. "Hey, I don't want you thinking I'm rude, Iris. It's just I need to be in touch with my people at all times. In this industry, you never know when a deal will break."

I'd half expected my dad would want to do something after lunch—go for a walk along Lake Champlain, wander through the mall at the other end of the parking lot—but he says he's tight for time; he needs to be in New York City for a dinner meeting. Something about getting together with an important investor and a side trip to Atlantic City.

Before we got to Friendly's, I was already planning excuses for why Mick and I wouldn't be able to stay in Plattsburgh. *I have an exam to study for. More lines to memorize. There'll be traffic at the border.*

When my father says he has to go, I'm relieved but also, somehow, disappointed.

My father acts insulted when Mick offers to pay the bill. "No way. It's mine." He puts his hand over the bill so Mick won't be able to take it. "It's the least I can do."

Then he reaches into his pocket. "I nearly forgot—I've got something for you, Iris." He takes out a small box wrapped in layers of pale green tissue paper. "The paper," he says softly, "it's the color of your eyes...and your mom's. I haven't asked—how is she?" It's hard to read the look in his eyes. Curiosity? Regret?

"She's fine. We're fine. She's busy with her business. She designs closets." That sounds better than saying she helps people get rid of their junk.

"That's good to hear." He doesn't ask me to send his regards. He must know I haven't told my mom about today.

He's right about the color of the tissue paper. I'm careful not to tear it. Inside the box is a silver ring with a dragon on it.

The dragon looks ferocious. Maybe because it has two red stones for eyes.

"It's a Thai good-luck ring," my father says. "In Thailand, the dragon is a symbol of strength."

He watches as I try on the ring. Lots of girls at school wear rings on their index fingers, but it slides right off that finger when I try it on. It's loose on my middle finger too.

"She'll have to have it sized," Mick says.

My ring finger has always been a little fatter than the rest, so I try it there next. It's a perfect fit. "Thank you," I tell my father. He'd probably like me to call him *Dad*, but I can't bring myself to do it. Not yet anyhow.

I do manage a stiff goodbye hug. "I'd like to try and be more of a father to you," he murmurs into my hair. "If you'll let me. About the acting, Iris. Go for it. Really go for it."

Back in the Jeep, I slump in my seat. Mick waits to turn on the engine. He runs his palm up and down my thigh. Gently. "You okay, Joey?"

I nod. It's hard for me to speak. There are too many feelings churning inside me—and they don't all make sense or fit together. I'm angry and I'm sad at the same time. I don't care if I ever see my father again; I want to know him better. He's a loser; he's not so bad. He's selfish; he's a dreamer. But he said he's proud of me—he said I should go for it. That counts for something. That counts for a lot.

Suddenly a memory comes back from a time I thought I had forgotten. I am a little girl, sitting on my father's lap. We're on the same corduroy couch that's still in our living room at home. He is singing to me. I can't remember the music or the words. Only the feeling of being happy.

I cry a little. For the things I once had and cannot remember, for the things I lost. And for Mick, because I'm so grateful he's here for me now. What would I do without him?

When he strokes my shoulder, I cry harder.

"That couldn't have been easy for you," Mick whispers. "But you did good, Joey."

When we're back on the highway, I twirl the dragon ring around and around my finger. The red stone eyes look flat until I turn my hand. When the light catches the stones, the dragon's eyes shimmer.

"That ring, by the way, has got to be the creepiest thing I've ever seen," Mick says.

I leave the ring on for a while. It's all I have from my father—that and the green tissue paper in my pocket. But Mick's right. The ring is creepy.

Before we cross back into Canada, I slide the ring off and drop it into my purse. It falls to the bottom without making a sound.

CHAPTER 12

"Though this be madness, yet there is method in 't."
—HAMLET, ACT 2, SCENE 2

I can hardly believe this is my life! It's too perfect!

Two weeks after our trip to Plattsburgh, Mick gave me the keys to the loft! Now I can go there whenever I want to, even if Mick is out. Mick wants to share his life with me. Why else would he have given me the keys?

I had to stop myself from jumping up and down like some little kid. The keys—there's a small silver one for the lobby door and a bigger gold one for upstairs—mean as much to me as that beautiful, beautiful poem Mick wrote for me. Even if he hasn't said out loud he loves me, I know he does, since he said so in the poem. Now I know for sure he loves me as much as I love him.

Though I've never been religious, I'm so grateful for Mick that I'm starting to think there really is a God.

Yesterday when I was alone in the loft, I actually dropped down on both knees and thanked him.

Thank you for making my heart glad. Thank you, God, if you're really up there, for bringing me Mick. Please help me try to be good enough and loving enough to deserve him. And God, while I have your attention, there's one more thing: please please stop me from saying or doing anything dumb that might make Mick angry with me—because I don't know what I'd do if he ever stopped loving me. I need Mick the way I need oxygen and food and a place to sleep.

Afterward, I just stood for a while in front of the windows, taking in the view of the city and feeling grateful. We'd had our first snow, and Montreal looked as if it'd been dusted in icing sugar.

⁓

The days end earlier this time of year. It's only four thirty now, and it's already getting dark. Mick is still at school, meeting with Ms. Cameron—I mean, Isobel—about *Hamlet*. He's put together a list of ways to make the production more relevant and edgy. I've noticed *edgy* is another one of Mick's favorite words.

I pick up some groceries on the way to the loft after school. I want to try and cook a romantic dinner.

When I let myself in, there is still a little light coming in from outside, which makes me notice dust I haven't seen before. So I drag the vacuum cleaner out of the closet and get to work. I even find the power nozzle so I can get into the corners.

It might not be cool to tidy up your boyfriend's loft, but I'm enjoying it. It makes me feel grown up, and like the loft's mine too. How amazing is that? To be seventeen and sharing a loft with your super cool, super sexy, edgy older boyfriend?

I turn off the vacuum cleaner when I see the movement of my phone vibrating on the table. Katie is texting to say she wants to meet up at Starbucks.

No can do, Kates, I text her back. Wrtng wrld hsty es-y.

Loser, Katie writes in her next text. Any news from Pop? Besides Mick, Katie is the only one who knows about my father. She thinks it's cool he contacted me, but she was ticked off when I told her I took the bus alone to Plattsburgh to meet him. "I can't believe you'd do that," she said. "That is so totally what a best friend is for. Plus we could've gone shopping together afterward. Makeup's way cheaper in the States."

No news, I text her. Since Plattsburgh, my father has sent me a couple of Facebook messages. Mostly he says how excited he is about the deal he's working on.

Katie doesn't text me back. When I start vacuuming again, I remember how when we were little, Katie and I sometimes played house or pretended we were in school. She always wanted to ride bikes or skip, but even back then, I was more into pretending. Maybe I was getting an early start on my acting career.

Vacuuming Mick's apartment and planning our romantic dinner (baked chicken with wild rice and a small green salad, like in a restaurant) feels like playing house again. Only now, it's real. Every time a dustball flies up from the floor and gets swallowed by the nozzle, I feel triumphant. Death to you, dustball!

I have to hurry. I want to put the vacuum cleaner away and get the chicken in the oven before Mick comes home. Mick keeps bringing me irises. The latest bouquet is in a glass milk jug on the table. The flowers are so pretty, I take a picture of them with my cell phone; I'll post it on my Facebook wall later. Maybe I'll even make the shot my profile picture. Irises for Iris.

I brush my hair away from my face. I don't want Mick to see me looking gross and sweaty. If I work quickly, I'll have time to shower and fix my makeup.

Mick bought me a toothbrush so I don't have to keep bringing mine over. Just seeing our two toothbrushes together in the bathroom, in the same cup, makes me want to sing or something.

By the time I hear Mick's key in the door, I am sitting on the couch, updating my Facebook page.

"Smells amazing in here," Mick calls out. I'm relieved his voice sounds happy. The meeting with Isobel must've gone well. I'm so tuned in to Mick's feelings, I can tell his mood just from his voice or the look in his eyes. If he's been arguing with his lawyer or someone from his Australian theater troupe, his voice and eyes turn steely. But I'm learning how to deal with him when he gets like that. I know it only makes things worse if I ask if there's anything I can do (and it's hard for me not to ask). No, the best thing is to take careful steps around him—it's like looking out for land mines in a war zone. You never know when you might step on one, but you get used to the not knowing and then it becomes a habit to step more carefully. Just in case. Mick is worth the trouble though. I'd be bored if I was with a guy whose mood never changed—who wasn't edgy the way Mick is.

Mick doesn't say anything about how clean the apartment is or how nice the table looks.

He does something even better. He kneels on the floor in front of where I'm sitting and starts kissing my knees. At first, it's just little kisses, but then the kisses get harder. "I'm starving," he whispers, and I know he's not talking about chicken and wild rice.

He's starving for *me*. With one hand, he pins my wrists against the wall; with the other, he tears off my underwear.

Then he's straddling me, pressing all his weight against me. It's a little uncomfortable, but I don't complain. I want to be in the moment with him. Besides, this is another way of feeling close to Mick. Everything about him is smooth. His skin, his touch, every move.

"Say your lines," he says. His voice is rough now, and I know it's because he's so excited.

He's remembering that first time we made love. I laugh because I know just what he wants. "'My lord,'" I whisper, "'as I was sewing in my closet, Lord Hamlet with his doublet all…'"

Even the little hairs on the outside of Mick's ears are standing up. He kisses me so hard, it makes my neck hurt.

I kiss him back. I want to bring my hand to my neck, to show Mick I need him to be gentle, but he's still got both my hands pinned against the wall. I'll try to forget the soreness in my neck.

"We shouldn't make too much noise," I whisper, suddenly aware of the wall behind us and of the sound of the TV coming from Mrs. Karpman's apartment. "We don't want to bother your neighbor."

"The old girl is deaf as a post. Besides, she could use a thrill."

When we're done, we snuggle on the couch, my head on Mick's shoulder. If I only lean in one direction, I don't feel the crick in my neck. I wish Mick would say he loves me, but I know I shouldn't ask him to. If I did and he did…well then, it wouldn't count, would it?

Mick never asks me how *it* was, the way Tommy did that time. In a way, I'm glad he doesn't, because I'm pretty sure I still haven't had an orgasm. Not that I care. I know I'll have one eventually. All that matters is that Mick and I are together.

Mick reaches for my laptop, which I've left open on the coffee table. "I like the picture of the irises," he says. His voice sounds relaxed and his face looks relaxed too. The tension I sometimes see around his eyes is gone. I love knowing I'm good for him. With Tommy, I never cared about stuff like that.

I should boil the water for the rice, but I don't want this moment to end. Ever. I wish Mick and I could stay like this forever. Mellow and happy, just the two of us.

Mick is scrolling down my Facebook wall. I know something's wrong when I feel his shoulder muscles get taut under my cheek. "What the fuck were you thinking, Iris?" It's the first time I've heard Mick swear. The word *fuck*, which always sounds ugly to me, sounds even uglier coming from him.

"What's wrong?" There's a sick, sour taste in my throat. I don't understand what could be making Mick so angry. I didn't see this land mine. All I did was change my profile picture.

"It says here you're in a relationship!" His voice is booming; it's as if he's acting in a small theater and he wants his voice to project. I need him to calm down. I need us to go back to how we were just two minutes ago. Mick is overreacting.

"I am in a relationship," I say quietly. "We are," I add.

"And what do we have here?" I've heard Mick shout before, but this is the first time I've seen him sneer. The sneer makes his nose look even longer, like a fox's snout. "Here it says you can't believe how 'tuned in' you feel to your new guy, *M*!" He sneers again when he says the words *tuned in*. I can tell he thinks it's a corny expression. Why did I ever write that?

"I didn't say your name. *M* could be..." I'm so rattled I can't even think of a guy's name that starts with an *M*. "Matthew!" I sputter. "Or Mark!"

"Iris! I can't believe you could be so reckless...so stupid." He spits out the word *stupid*. Mick is right. I am stupid. So what if I get good grades in every subject at school? In real life, I'm stupid! The stupidest girl who ever walked the earth! I should've known Mick would be upset.

"I'm sorry," I manage to say. I don't want to cry, but I feel the tears building up inside my head like a drain that's clogged and is about to burst.

Mick grabs my wrists again. This time, I know it's not because he wants to make love. I try to move away, but I'm not quick enough. "Let go!" I say, trying to shake myself loose.

I see Mick's palm, open like a fan, coming at me—and then he does something I would never have expected. Not in a billion years. Mick smacks me. Not the wall this time. Me. My face. My cheek. It happens quickly, so I have the weird sense I'm watching the scene unfold from a distance. As if there are two Irises. The good Iris—the one who makes Mick happy. The bad Iris—the stupid one who keeps screwing things up.

Bad Iris crumples to the floor like a toy that's lost its stuffing and can't stand upright. Her cheek burns.

The other Iris, the good one, just watches. She's afraid to make a sound. If she does, Mick might get even angrier.

Mick's right.

I'm reckless and stupid.

When he sees me run my hand over my cheek, he doesn't try to comfort me. He doesn't apologize either. Instead, he stomps over to the little kitchen. I watch him as he opens the oven door, then slams it shut. "It looks like the chicken's nearly done," he says.

CHAPTER 13

"Rich gifts wax poor when givers prove unkind."
—*HAMLET*, ACT 3, SCENE 1

I cry a little in the bathroom. But mostly I press a cold washcloth to my cheek. The skin is raised and red and warm to the touch where Mick smacked me. I should never have changed my status on Facebook. I should have known Mick would lose it if he found out. I should've remembered how private he is—and how much he has to lose. Things'll be different once I graduate. I know they will be. Then we won't have to hide our relationship. And Mick and I won't have anything left to fight about.

I take my time in the bathroom. Partly because I need to regroup, but mostly because I'm expecting Mick to come and get me, to say he's sorry and to promise he'll never ever hurt me again. Because he *has* hurt me. My cheek still stings, and even with the cold compress, the skin is swelling up. Hopefully no one'll notice. If anyone does,

I'll have to come up with some excuse. I can say someone accidentally whacked me during Theater Workshop. That'll work, especially since Ms. Cameron gave us that warm-up exercise where we slapped each other.

Mick doesn't come to get me, so in the end, I go to him.

I know I probably shouldn't, that I should wait for him to come to me. But I can't stand us being in a fight. I need for things to go back to how they were.

Mick's trying in his own way to make it up to me. I know he is because he's put the chicken on our plates and he's sliced carrots into perfect rounds. He's waiting at the table, his cloth napkin tucked into the collar of his shirt like a bib.

If he notices my cheek is puffy, he doesn't mention it. I know it's because he's too upset to talk about what happened. I understand how he feels. I want to forget what happened too. I want to forget how much I upset him. How stupid and careless I was. I need to try harder not to upset Mick—especially when he's already under so much pressure. If only I could take it all back and start over again.

"After supper, I'll change my status on Facebook." My voice cracks, but I don't let myself cry. I know if I cry, it'll only make Mick more upset. I don't want him to feel guilty about what happened. I had it coming to me.

Mick holds his fork like a spear as he cuts into his piece of chicken. "I've already gone ahead and changed it. And I deleted that last ridiculous post on your wall too."

I'm about to ask Mick how he knew my password when I realize I never shut down my laptop. "Thanks," I say softly. I don't say what I'm thinking: I bet he'd go ballistic if I messed around on his computer.

"Chicken's good," he says, wiping his lips with his napkin. "Nice and moist."

"I marinated it in Italian salad dressing. The store-bought kind. I saw the recipe on the bottle and I thought it looked good. It's low-fat." I'm babbling, but I can't stop. I don't want there to be empty air between us. I'm trying to act as if everything's normal. It's the only thing I can think of to make things better.

Mick hasn't even looked at my cheek. I hope that means the swelling isn't so bad. "Hey," he says, "I nearly forgot. I've got a nice bottle of Australian chardonnay chilling in the fridge." He gets up from the table to get the wine and the wineglasses. "When you come to Australia," he says from the kitchen, "we'll tour the vineyards. I want to introduce you to some New World wines, Joey."

My heart flutters when he says that. So he isn't upset with me anymore! Why else would he talk about my coming to Australia and visiting vineyards with him?

I know it's Mick's way of saying he's sorry. "I'd love that," I tell him. When I feel myself starting to choke up, I swallow to make the feeling go away. I don't want to cry—even if it's crying from relief. Mick and I are going to be able to get past what happened to us earlier.

I take a small sip of the wine Mick pours for me. I'm thinking how terrible he must feel and how I'd do anything to make things between us good again. Anything.

"Let's toast," Mick says, lifting his glass into the air.

"To us," I say hopefully.

"To theater!" Mick says. I watch his eyes as we clink wineglasses. The dark pools are calm again. I'm so relieved he's not angry anymore. Still, I wish he'd wanted to toast us, not theater. But now isn't the right time to mention it.

"I'm sorry," I whisper instead.

Mick looks surprised. For a moment, I wish I hadn't reminded him of our argument. He looks over my head. "Let's get past that, Joey," he says.

He's right, of course. In a good relationship, you need to get past the difficult moments—the blips that are bound to happen. Getting through hard times will bring us even closer.

For a while, we both just eat our chicken. "I meant to make rice," I tell Mick, "only I didn't get around to it."

If Mick realizes he had something to do with why I didn't get around to making rice, he doesn't let on.

"Rice would've been good," he says, "though you know I like to watch my carbs." He pats his belly. It's as flat as a teenager's.

Mick tops up our glasses. The wine helps me relax. He leans back in his chair. "Good theater," he says, "is about lying."

I don't know where that comment came from, but I'm glad we're talking about theater and not about us or the argument we had. I lean back in my chair too. "Lying? What do you mean?"

"The lie starts as soon as the audience comes into the theater space. We're asking people to check their disbelief at the door, along with their coats and, if it's raining, their umbrellas." Mick chuckles at his own joke.

That makes me laugh too. It feels good to laugh. So light, so free. I love Mick's sense of humor—the way he says funny things in a deadpan way so that if you didn't know him the way I do, you might miss the joke altogether.

Mick tilts his glass and examines the color of the wine. "Great actors are great liars," he says.

"I'm not a very good liar." I'm thinking how hard it's been to lie to my mom and Katie. Sometimes I think I need a notebook to keep track of all the lies I've been telling.

"You know what great actors and great liars have in common?" Mick asks me.

"I don't know. Tell me."

Mick leans back on his chair. I know he likes telling me things. "Empathy. A great actor inhabits the character he's playing. Years ago in London, I saw Anthony Hopkins playing Lear. And that's exactly what Hopkins did. He *was* Lear. A great liar has to get inside the mind of the person he's lying to. So he'll know exactly what that person wants to hear."

"I'm confused," I say. "Isn't the whole point of art—any art—to tell the truth?"

"You're right, Joey. " (I can't help feeling proud when Mick says I'm right. See, I think to myself, I am smart—about some things anyway.) "That is the point of art. To raise people's consciousness, especially about difficult subjects. To make them reflect on their own lives and society. But sometimes, it takes a lie to convey the truth."

I'm still confused. Maybe it's the wine—it's making me light-headed. I reach for Mick's hand across the little table. For a moment, I worry he won't let me take it, that maybe he's not over our fight yet—but he does. "I really love talking to you about this stuff," I tell him.

"Me too, Joey," he says. "Me too."

CHAPTER 14

"Friends to this ground."
—*HAMLET*, ACT 1, SCENE 1

M om leaves for work at seven, so there's time for me to phone my father before school. It's already evening in Bangkok. He knows I'll be calling because I messaged him on Facebook. I told him I had something I needed to ask him and that I didn't want to ask it over Facebook.

"Iris!" he says when he picks up. It's as if I can hear him smiling. "How's everything going over there?"

I need to swallow before I answer. "Great. Everything's great."

"And the play? How's that coming?"

"It's getting a little better with every rehearsal. Thanks for asking." I nearly call him *Dad*, but I stop myself.

"So what do you need to ask me?"

This is harder than I expected. I take a deep breath. "Was naming me Iris really your idea?"

"It sure was. Don't tell me that's what you couldn't ask me over Facebook." His voice is gentle. He must know I'm working my way up to the real question.

I take an even deeper breath. "If what you said is true and my mom wouldn't let you see me..." I'm finding it hard to go on. To formulate the question. But I don't have to.

"Oh, Iris," he says, and now I know he isn't smiling. "You want to know why she prevented me from contacting you...that's it, isn't it?"

I can barely say, "Uh-huh."

"I'm sorry, Iris, I really am." I know from his voice that he means it. "But your mom's the only one who can answer that question. You're going to have to ask her." He pauses. "When you're ready."

I can't stop thinking about the phone call. Not even when I'm in Theater Workshop and, later, in Economics class. Why won't my father tell me what happened—and will I ever be ready to ask my mom?

The Economics teacher calls my name twice before I look up. "Iris, can you answer the question, please?"

"Uh, I'm sorry...but I don't think I heard it."

Lenore's arm shoots up. "I think the term you're looking for is the law of diminishing returns."

"I'm glad to know some of you are paying attention," the teacher says.

Lenore turns her head just enough to give me a condescending smile.

After school, Katie and I hurry along Monkland Avenue, on our way to the Villa-Maria metro station. Our arms are linked, and we keep our heads down to protect our faces from the gusty November wind. "I can't believe you couldn't answer that question about decreasing returns," Katie says.

"Diminishing. Not decreasing."

Katie doesn't seem to notice that I've corrected her.

"You know what else I can't believe? That you didn't take a picture of him! You should've known I'd want to see what he looks like."

"I know it's dumb, but I only thought about it afterward," I tell her. "He sent me a picture on Facebook—I'll show you that later. You'll see he looks like me. I mean, I look like him. Same cheekbones, same wide-apart eyes. And we have the same laugh. He's taller than I expected, and handsome. Well, kind of. I can sort of see why Mom fell for him."

I can almost feel Katie shiver under her jacket. "You still haven't told her about Plattsburgh?"

"I don't think she could handle it. Did I tell you he used to act?"

"That's pretty cool. So maybe acting's in your genes."

"She could've told me."

Katie knows I mean my mom. "So are you happier now that you've seen him and he's your Facebook friend?"

We're crossing Girouard Avenue. At least it'll be warm inside the station. "Do I seem happier?"

Katie does something unusual for her. She stops to think about the question. "You seem different. Not necessarily happier. But definitely different. You're not hanging out with Mick what's-his-name, are you?"

I can't believe Katie has just asked me that. It's a good thing she can't see my face.

"Of course not." I figure I should go on the offensive. "Why would you ask me such a weird question?"

"Antoine said he thought he saw you two—at the mountain. In a pedal boat."

"In a pedal boat? That's insane! Hey, I thought you said Antoine was dead to you."

"He is," Katie says. "Usually anyway."

The metro is late. Katie grabs my arm. "D'you think there was a jumper?"

"Do you have to call them *jumpers*?"

I hate the dirty-socks smell of Montreal's underground city. But as long as there are no mechanical difficulties—and no suicides (what Katie calls *jumpers*)—you can usually set your watch by our metro system.

It was my idea to take Katie downtown shopping. I want to buy us friendship bracelets. I told Katie I wanted to make it up to her for missing her party and for saying no the last few times she wanted to go for coffee. "I'm over it, Iris. I know how obsessed you get when you're writing a paper for English. It totally sucked that you missed my party, but hey, your mom had food poisoning. It's not like you could've abandoned her. Not when it was coming out both ends," Katie said.

"It was pretty gross."

I'm getting better at lying. Probably because I'm getting so much practice. But I still don't enjoy it. Mostly because I'm worried I'll screw up and let the truth slip out. I don't worry about that happening when I'm onstage. Onstage, lying's allowed.

I see the white headlights of a metro car coming down the tunnel. The car pulls up, the silver doors slide open, and Katie and I grab facing seats.

"Can you imagine ever being so depressed you'd jump in front of a metro?" Katie can be kind of morbid sometimes—and loud too. "Just like that. Splat." She smacks her thigh to demonstrate.

"I can't imagine. I think the people who do it must have serious mental problems. They're not just regular depressed."

"I guess it'd be over quickly," Katie says. "That's probably the appeal."

"Yeah, but think of all the people you'd traumatize. The ones who saw your splattered remains." When I'm with Katie, I get a little morbid too.

"Even worse," Katie says, shaking her head, "think of all the people who'd be late for their appointments downtown, all because of your splattered remains."

I shouldn't laugh. It's a bad joke. But it is funny, so I do. Katie bumps her knee against mine. For a minute, it feels like nothing's changed between us. I bump knees back.

"I miss you, Iris," Katie says out of nowhere.

I'm afraid to look at her when she says that. Afraid she'll know I've been keeping something from her. "I miss you too," I say to my clunky black boots.

"Has it ever occurred to you," Katie asks, "that maybe you study too much?"

"Has it ever occurred to you that maybe you study too little?"

Katie rolls her eyes. "Nope, that's never occurred to me."

She only brings up Facebook when we're transferring at the Lionel-Groulx terminus. So much for my hoping she hasn't been online. "I saw you changed your status to *In a relationship* and then you changed it back to *Single*. What's up with that? Don't tell me you gave Tommy another chance!" Katie has never had a very high opinion of Tommy. "I would so never give Antoine another chance."

"Then how come you two are back on speaking terms?"

"That's different. We don't do much speaking."

"Katie!"

It could be worse. Katie must not have seen what I wrote about feeling tuned in to "M."

"I kind of did give Tommy another chance," I tell her.

"I thought you hated him."

"I never said I hated him. I just said I wasn't in love with him."

"You really need to come out dancing with me one of these nights," Katie says. "It'd be good for you."

How can I tell Katie that going clubbing with a bunch of silly underage teenage girls trying to act grown up is the last thing I'm interested in? They go to clubs to meet guys, and I've already met the perfect guy. If anything, I feel sorry for Katie. What if she never meets anyone who makes her feel the way Mick makes me feel?

"You'd have totally loved the after-hours club we went to Saturday. I didn't get home till ten in the morning."

"You must've been wrecked. What'd you tell your parents?"

Katie nudges me. "What do you think I told them? That I slept over at your house."

Thank God our moms don't compare notes. Katie's mom gets her hair blown out every week and has long lunches with her girlfriends at expensive restaurants downtown. My mom's too busy working to worry about her hair. And she's really careful with money.

"Which club did you go to?" I don't ask because I'm interested, but because I know Katie is dying to tell me. It's like someone asking me how it feels to be onstage. Clubbing is Katie's passion. Mick says everyone should have a passion. That if we follow our passions, we'll always be headed in the right direction.

"It's called Circus. I'll bet you never even heard of it, right? It's in the Gay Village. The music was awesome, techno mostly. We never stopped dancing." Katie's eyes are shining. All I can think about is how tired I'd feel if I stayed up all night. Were Katie and I ever in the same world?

Katie is just getting warmed up. "There's usually a twenty-dollar cover charge, but they let us in for free. The bouncer said, 'Pretty girls bring in business.'" Katie laughs when she imitates the bouncer. "The place was packed."

"Wow!" I try to sound excited. "Hey, d'you know any rice recipes?"

"Rice recipes?" Katie peels off one of her gloves and makes a show of feeling my forehead. "Are you all right, Iris?" You'd think I'd told her I was pregnant with triplets.

"Most people just boil water and add the rice. But I think there are better ways to do it. I meant to look online. Did you ever—"

"Did I ever research rice recipes? Who do you think I am—Martha friggin' Stewart? You really need to get a life, Iris. I swear, sometimes I think you're turning into some old lady. Going to bed early, studying nonstop and now, talking about rice recipes. Don't you ever just want to be seventeen?"

I don't tell Katie what I'm thinking: No, I don't ever just want to be seventeen. Not anymore. Not since I met Mick.

Accessories are on the ground floor at H&M. I like the pink and silver bracelets—they'd go with everything—but Katie chooses one with turquoise crystals. "It's more fun than the pink." I know she's found another way to say I'm turning into a little old lady.

So I end up buying two turquoise bracelets. When the salesclerk asks if I want them wrapped, Katie says, "We're gonna wear them. They're friendship bracelets." She slips hers on, holding it up to the fluorescent lighting so the crystals shimmer. "We've been besties since pre-school." Katie squeezes my elbow.

I slip mine on too. I wish I'd bought the pink.

"Listen," Katie says when we're leaving H&M, "Lenore was gonna be downtown this afternoon. I said we'd meet up with her for a bubble tea."

"You did? Since when did you start hanging out with Lenore?"

"She came to Circus with us on Saturday. She was actually pretty cool."

"I need to get home. To make that rice. It's for my mom. Ever since that business with the food poisoning, she's been trying to eat light." My lie is starting to feel real.

"I totally love my bracelet, Iris." Katie twirls her wrist. "Call me later, okay? Promise?" She blows me an air kiss. I can feel her looking over my head—probably for Lenore.

"I promise," I tell her. Only I know I won't.

CHAPTER 15

"What a piece of work is a man!...
In action how like an angel..."
—*HAMLET*, ACT 2, SCENE 2

Mick's right.

I'm outgrowing Katie. He says it's part of life—like a child outgrowing a pair of pants. "They were a fine pair of pants, but they don't fit you anymore. They're too small for the person you are becoming," he said. Mick also says it takes courage to let some relationships go. Still, I miss Katie.

"How do I know you won't outgrow me?" Almost as soon as the question was out of my mouth, I was sorry I'd asked it. I hate sounding insecure.

Mick didn't seem to mind. "That could never happen, Joey," he said (I got little shivers when he said that). Then he took my hands and pressed them to his chest, over his heart. "We're soulmates, Joey. This is destiny."

I love how that sounds. *Soulmates. This is destiny.* Still, I wish I knew whether Mick had that feeling with anyone else before me. Did he have it with Nial's mother—the woman he cut out of the photograph? But I don't ask. Maybe because I don't really want to know the answer.

My shift at Scoops is nearly over. It's a wonder people still want ice cream on such a wintery day. I'm looking out the window just as Mick's Jeep pulls up at the corner. It's snowing, and his windshield wipers are going double time. Phil looks up from the cash as I leave. "I'm glad you've got a ride. If you don't mind my asking, who's that guy who keeps coming to get you?"

"He's just a friend."

Phil drums his fingers on the counter. "From what I can tell, he looks a little old to be your friend."

"He isn't." I hope that'll shut Phil up, but it doesn't.

"How come he never comes inside?"

"I don't know. I'll ask him. See ya, Phil."

When I get in the Jeep and Mick kisses me hard on the lips, I forget Phil, the demanding customers, the after-dinner rush and the squishy sound my nurse's shoes made all afternoon as I flew across the restaurant's sticky floor.

"We're making a quick stop." Mick's voice doesn't give anything away.

"What for?"

Mick puts a finger to his lips. It's another surprise! I smile—not just with my lips but inside too. Mick's more fun than anyone I've ever known. He turns life into a game. It's another thing I love about him. It's also why I miss him so much when we're apart. On weeknights, when I go back to Mom's, everything there feels flat and dull. Like my world's in black and white, not color, the way it is when I'm with Mick.

Mick pulls up in front of a stone townhouse on a pretty street tucked away behind the Montreal Museum of Fine Arts. "We're going to stop in to see Marilyn—she's a friend of Isobel's. She has something for us."

I reach for Mick's hand as we trudge along the path to the house, but he won't hold hands. That must mean Isobel's friend isn't supposed to know about us.

Before we can ring the bell, a tall woman with hair like gray straw opens the door. She doesn't say a word, just takes our coats and gestures for us to follow her inside.

"Here they are," she whispers. There's a fire crackling in the fireplace in her living room. In front of the fireplace is a round wicker basket. Inside it is a sleek marmalade cat with three tiny kittens—one calico, two marmalade like their mom—curled around her. Two other kittens, just as small but black, come racing across the wooden floor, running sideways the way kittens do.

The sleeping kittens are rolled into fuzzy snail balls. One of the marmalade ones opens a yellow eye, looks right at me and yawns.

"I asked Iris here to come along and help me pick out a kitten," Mick tells the straw-haired woman.

"Are we really getting a kitten?" I squeal, but then I correct myself. "Are *you* really getting a kitten, Mick?"

"I'm really getting a kitten."

Marilyn puts her hands on her hips and looks at Mick. "It's important to me that these kittens go to good homes. So I need to know what'll happen to the kit if you go back to Australia. Isobel told me you're from there."

"Let's just say at the moment there's a lot keeping me here." Mick doesn't look at me when he says this—I know he can't—but I know he means me, that I'm keeping him in Montreal. My heart swells with pleasure.

"How do you two know each other exactly?" Marilyn asks. For a moment, her eyes narrow like the marmalade cat's.

"Iris is one of Isobel's star students. I spotted her waiting at the bus stop. The snow was coming down pretty hard on the poor kid, so I offered her a ride." Mick's a much better liar than I am. Still, I don't like him calling me a *kid*.

"Well then, Iris," Mick says. "Which one do you like?"

The two black kittens are frisky and beautiful. The calico in the basket is purring like a small engine.

But it's the marmalade yawner I think I want. When I lean close to the basket, he stretches out one paw in my direction, as if he's asking for my help.

"It looks like this little guy likes you," Mick says. I feel bad for taking the kitten from his mom, but when I scoop him up, he doesn't object. Instead, he settles into the crook of my arm and licks the inside of my elbow. His little pink tongue makes me laugh.

"I've got some kitten food to get you started. You'll need to buy a litter box," Marilyn says. "I'm glad to see him go to a good home."

Marilyn watches from the doorway as Mick and I head back to the Jeep. I'm holding our new kitten inside my coat. Mick walks several feet ahead of us. He doesn't notice when I nearly slip on an icy patch.

"Look out for yourself, Iris," Marilyn calls out.

"What are you going to name him?" Mick asks when we're back in the Jeep. The kitten is still curled up inside my coat.

"I haven't decided yet."

I wait in the car while Mick goes into the pet store. From the parking lot, I can look through the store windows. Mick is carrying a giant box of cat litter. His cheeks are rosy from the cold. When he sees me watching him, he waves a feathery cat toy at me. I'm careful not to laugh. I don't want to wake the kitten.

He makes a little snoring sound. He's our kitten. Mine and Mick's. I promise myself that we'll give this little guy a good home—a safe, calm place where he won't be too lonely for the rest of his family.

That's when I come up with his name. William Shakespeare. And I'll ask Mick not to call him by a nickname the way he does with me.

He'll be William Shakespeare because he's smart and noble and by calling him that, he'll always remind Mick and me of the day we met.

Someone's tapping on the car window. The tapping wakes William Shakespeare. His little ears twitch back and forth. "It's okay," I tell him, "go back to sleep."

The person doing the tapping is dressed in jogging gear. When he pulls up his navy balaclava, I see it's Tommy. What's he doing out in this weather?

"Iris," he says when I roll down the window, "I thought it was you." His eyelashes have snow on them. "Nice Jeep. Whose is it?"

"A friend's."

Now he notices William Shakespeare nestled inside my coat. One of the kitten's eyes is closed; the other is on Tommy. "I didn't know you had a cat," Tommy says.

"We—I just got him. I better roll up the window now. I don't want him getting cold. Be careful out there," I tell Tommy. "It's slippery."

Tommy adjusts his balaclava before he jogs back out to the street. I watch as the reflective stripes on the back of his pants get farther and farther away.

A few minutes later, Mick opens the back door of the Jeep and tosses in the things he's bought. He doesn't mention Tommy. He must have been at the cash when Tommy stopped to talk to me.

"Meet William Shakespeare," I tell Mick.

"It's a good name," he says. "Nice to meet you, Bill."

"Not Bill," I say in my firmest voice. I'm not used to standing up to Mick. "William Shakespeare."

The streets are getting slushy, especially at the intersections. Mick speeds up to make it through a yellow light, and a wave of gray slush splashes into the air. I see Tommy on the sidewalk, jogging on the spot and shaking his head. Mick has just drenched him.

Mick doesn't seem to notice what he's done—and though I feel bad for Tommy, I figure it's better not to mention it.

I pet the soft spot between William Shakespeare's ears.

"If you keep cuddling up with that bloke," Mick says, "you're gonna make me jealous."

I laugh. I also release my hold on William Shakespeare. He opens one eye as if to say, "Now why in the world would you do that?"

CHAPTER 16

"He was a man. Take him for all in all.
I shall not look upon his like again."
—*HAMLET*, ACT 1, SCENE 2

The needles are falling off the Christmas tree in the lobby of Mick's building. The packages underneath—some wrapped in shiny Christmas paper, others in blue-and-white Hanukkah paper—are getting dusty. I'm wearing the vintage wool coat Mick surprised me with for Christmas. So what if the fox collar tickles my neck? It makes me feel like a movie star.

When I let myself into the lobby, Mrs. Karpman is there, waiting for the elevator. She is surrounded by shopping bags. "I can't resist the January sales," she explains. "I already bought the children presents for Hanukkah next year." She insists on showing me the turtleneck sweater she bought for her eldest grandson.

I help Mrs. Karpman with her bags. I can't say no when she invites me in for tea. I try telling her I want to do some studying before Mick gets back, but she insists. "Just a quick cup of tea, Iris. I do so want you to meet Sunshine."

Only with Mrs. Karpman, nothing happens quickly. She wants me to choose a teacup from her extensive teacup collection. "That one's bone china," she says when I choose a cup and saucer with dusty-rose cabbage leaves on it. "Nelson bought it for me when we were in London in 1965. It was a marvelous trip. Next time I'll show you the album."

Sunshine lives in a small cage by the window in Mrs. Karpman's kitchen. He's egg-yolk yellow with a sharp orange beak, and when he sings, he makes a happy trill.

"Only the boys sing," Mrs. Karpman tells me as she pours my tea. "If you put a female canary into a cage with a male one, he stops singing."

I don't have the heart to tell Mrs. Karpman that maybe Sunshine is singing from loneliness. For a moment, I remember how I felt before I met Mick—as if I'd never find anyone who really *got* me. I'd have sung, too, if I'd thought it could help me meet someone like him.

I tell Mrs. Karpman about William Shakespeare. She says she'd like to meet him sometime too. "Though, to be honest, I have more of an affinity for birds than cats." She looks over at Sunshine when she says that. The canary is swinging back and forth on his wooden perch.

Mrs. Karpman relaxes into her velvet armchair and sips her tea. "Loneliness is a dreadful thing," she says. The comment seems to come out of nowhere. Will I do that too when I am old?

"How long has it been since Mr. Karpman—Nelson—died?" I ask, hoping the question won't make Mrs. Karpman miss him even more. But she looks pleased that I've remembered her husband's name.

"It's been fifteen years," she tells me, looking into her teacup as if she can see Nelson's reflection there. "He was considerably older than me. A little like you and that Australian charmer of yours."

"The age difference doesn't matter to us," I say quickly. "We're interested in all the same things. Mick's a theater director; I want to act."

"Nelson and I had a great deal in common too. We both loved to travel. And he was a wonderful father. He changed diapers and helped with the feedings. In our day, there weren't many men who did those things. Do you suppose your Mick will make a good father?" I can feel Mrs. Karpman's eyes watching my face as she waits for my answer.

"He already has a son. A little boy named Nial. He's in Australia with his mother. They're divorced—Mick and Nial's mother, I mean." Somehow, though I hardly know her, Mrs. Karpman's opinion matters to me.

I don't want her to think I'd have a relationship with a married man.

"How old is the little boy?" she asks.

"Almost two."

"He must miss his daddy," she says, sighing.

"What about your kids?" I ask, eager to change the subject. "Are they in Montreal?" If they are, they don't come to see her very often. In all the times I've been at Mick's, I've never heard or seen any visitors next door.

"My son and daughter are both in Toronto. And I've got five delicious grandchildren." She says the word *delicious* like she's describing a cinnamon Danish, not people. "The eldest, Errol, what a doll that boy is. He might be coming to McGill next fall. Now that would be a blessing. He says he'll come for Friday-night dinners because no one makes a roast chicken like his bubbie."

"Did you ever think of moving to Toronto—to be closer to them all?"

Mrs. Karpman looks around her little kitchen and smiles. "I try to get to Toronto whenever I can. In fact, I'm going next month. But no, I'd never move away from Montreal. I couldn't bear to leave Nelson behind."

"But Nelson's dead," I say softly. For the first time, I wonder if maybe Mrs. Karpman is so old she's getting senile.

"Nelson and I lived together in this apartment for twenty-two years. I feel his spirit everywhere all the time.

He dried the dishes at that sink. And he put up that shelf for me—for my salt-and-pepper-shaker collection." I look over at the shelf, which is jammed with shakers. I'm sure that, like Mrs. Karpman's teacups, each pair of shakers has a story and that if I asked, Mrs. Karpman would be only too happy to tell me all of them. "He's buried in Montreal too—at the Mount Royal Cemetery."

I can't imagine relying on a dead person for company.

I set my teacup down on the table and walk over to the birdcage. Sunshine is pacing on the bar of his wooden swing. When I make a kissing sound, he jumps off the swing and grabs onto the cage bars with his scaly feet. He's staring right at me now.

"I think Sunshine likes you," Mrs. Karpman says approvingly.

She wants to show me some photos in her living room. There is one of just Nelson and several of the two of them together. Nelson has a broad moon face and hardly any hair. In the photo, he is holding a gold pocket watch. "I took that one of Nelson," Mrs. Karpman says, pointing to the portrait. "He was always fiddling with that watch. Setting it and resetting it, checking the time. I bought it for him when he turned fifty. I had the jeweler engrave it with the letter *N*. Nelson always kept it with him. He said it reminded him of me." She sniffles when she says that.

"I'm sorry," I whisper. I don't know what else to say.

Mrs. Karpman taps the glass over a photo of the two of them. A much younger Mrs. Karpman beams as she holds on tightly to her husband's arm, as if she's afraid he might take off.

"Did you two always get along?" I ask. It's strange that of everyone I know, Mrs. Karpman is the only one I can talk to about my relationship with Mick.

When she pats my hand, I get the feeling that although she's hard of hearing, she's heard Mick and me fighting. I feel my cheeks heating up in shame. "No two people always get along." I know she is choosing her words carefully. "I think Nelson and I squabbled more in our early days together. It's all part of getting used to each other."

I nod. What Mrs. Karpman has just said makes so much sense. Mick and I have been squabbling too. That's exactly the right word. A squabble isn't as bad as a fight. Mick and I squabble sometimes because we're still getting used to each other. *No two people always get along.*

"One thing though—I always knew Nelson respected me." Mrs. Karpman watches my face when she says this, as if she's weighing whether to say more.

I nod again. Mick is always saying how much potential I have as an actress and how beautiful he thinks I am. That's respect, isn't it?

"Sometimes," Mrs. Karpman says, "a woman needs to stand up for herself and demand respect."

"I'd never need to do that with Mick."

I don't like that Mrs. Karpman is making me feel I have to defend my own boyfriend. She must realize I'm offended, because she changes the subject. "Now let me show you the grandchildren," she says as she directs me to another wall of photos. There, I see all five grandchildren, photographed at every age and in various combinations. With each other, with their parents, alone on baby blankets, and posed against blue backgrounds, with their hands folded, in school photos.

"That's Errol," Mrs. Karpman says, tapping her finger on a chrome frame. "Have you ever seen such a good-looking boy? That turtleneck is going to look so good on him!"

I say yes, Errol is handsome, but the truth is, I hardly look at the photograph. There is only one good-looking man I want to look at. In that way I guess I'm a little like Mrs. Karpman. I'll never stop loving Mick, just like she's never stopped loving Nelson. That thought makes me forgive her for hinting that maybe Mick isn't right for me.

"I'll drop by again," I tell her. Even if Mrs. Karpman is a little nosy, I'd still like to invite her to meet William Shakespeare. Only I don't think Mick would want an unexpected visitor. It'd be better, I think, to invite her to come sometime when he isn't there.

"I'm going to the seniors' center to play mahjong with some friends this afternoon," Mrs. Karpman tells me when she takes me to the door. "Nelson hated mahjong. He didn't see the point of it. You know, dear"—Mrs. Karpman drops her voice as if she's about to let me in on a great secret—"it's not always so terrible to be alone. Nelson, bless his soul, could get a little bossy sometimes. And now, well, I'm my own boss." Her pale eyes twinkle when she says that.

Mrs. Karpman kisses me on both cheeks. "I've just thought of something, Iris. Would you mind looking after Sunshine when I go to Toronto next month? You'd just have to freshen up his birdseed and give him water. I'd pay you, of course."

"I'd be glad to do it—and I wouldn't want any money." Somehow, I like the idea of sitting by myself in Mrs. Karpman's apartment with just Sunshine for company.

Mrs. Karpman wants me to take the spare key she keeps on a hook behind the door. "So you'll have it when I'm away," she says. An Eiffel Tower ornament dangles from the keychain. It must be a souvenir from one of the Karpmans' trips. There's also a little ID tag on the keychain. In neat, bold letters, it says *KARPMAN*.

CHAPTER 17

"The native hue of resolution
Is sicklied o'er with the pale cast of thought..."
—HAMLET, ACT 3, SCENE 1

I've spread out the college brochures on Mick's coffee table. Every one is plastered with photos of happy teenagers who have no trouble making decisions. It's as if there are thirty faces smirking at me from the glossy sheets, all asking the same question: *What's wrong with you, Iris Wagner?*

I have to decide which college I'm going to apply to for next September and what program I want to go into. I've got brochures from four colleges—one private, three public. I'll have to pay tuition at the private college, but the classes are smaller and the school has a good reputation. One of the public colleges is on the metro line, so that'd make it easier to get to school for early classes. As for programs, I need to choose between Arts and Science, Arts or Science, Creative Arts or Social Science. My head hurts from trying to keep track of all the options.

Like Hamlet, I'm terrible at making decisions. I think it's because I worry I'll end up regretting whatever I decide. When I was little, I used to take forever to choose a chocolate bar or a flavor of ice cream. If I chose butter-scotch, I'd wonder as soon as I took the first lick if maybe the double fudge would've tasted even better. I know a person is supposed to be able to make a decision and live with it, but that's not how it works for me. I come close to making a decision, then change my mind, then wonder if the first decision would've been the better one.

I wish I could be more like Katie. I've never seen her hesitate when it comes to choosing chocolate bars or ice cream. Katie's already been accepted into the Artistic Makeup program at Inter-Dec College.

Our guidance counselor, Ms. Odette, isn't much help. Besides handing me a packet of brochures, she gave me an online aptitude test that showed I had a talent for languages and communication but that I was also good with numbers. "What about accounting, Iris?" she'd asked me, which made me want to strangle her. Me? An accoun-tant? I don't think so.

When I told Ms. Odette I want to be an actor, she said I should follow my heart. But in the next breath she advised me to be practical. "In this day and age, Iris, a woman needs to be independent and able to support herself." I nodded my head, but all the while I was thinking that I didn't want to end up like Ms. Odette. She might be independent and self-supporting, but she wears way too much perfume and has a permanently sour look on her face—as if she thinks life should have treated her better than it has.

Of course, Mom's all for being practical. I still haven't found a way to talk to her about my father; talking to her about school is easier. "I'm not saying you're not talented," she told me over dinner last night, "but in my opinion, acting is more a hobby than a career."

"What about Meryl Streep?" I asked, knowing she's Mom's all-time favorite actor.

Mom sighed. "Meryl Streep is Meryl Streep," she said, as if that explained everything. "How about a little more pasta?"

I try writing a list of pros and cons. That was Ms. Odette's suggestion. But it doesn't work. When I start with a list of pros and cons about the private college, both sides have the exact same number of points. Rather than helping me clarify my thoughts, the way Ms. Odette said it would, the list only makes me feel more distressed. I hate myself for being so indecisive!

William Shakespeare is sitting next to me on the couch. I wish he'd tell me what to do. I scratch the orange triangle over his nose and he makes a contented purr. Sometimes I wish I were a cat. Then my biggest decision would be whether to sit on the couch or by the window. Knowing me, I'd have trouble with that too.

"At least I didn't have trouble choosing you," I tell him. And then I remember the afternoon we got him and how Mick pointed out that William Shakespeare chose me. It's a wonder, I think, that I was able to choose Mick. But then again, I didn't have much choice about that either. Mick's right: we were destined to be together.

But what college am I destined for? And what program? Why shouldn't I follow my dream? Then again, what if I don't make it as an actor? Most people don't. What then? I feel dizzy from thinking so hard. Where is destiny now that I need it?

I am rereading the brochures—it must be the fifteenth time—when Mick comes in. "What's for supper?" he calls out. "I could eat a horse."

"I forgot all about supper. Sorry," I add, not because I really am sorry (why do I have to be in charge of supper?) but because I don't want to set Mick off. The negotiations with Nial's mother haven't been going well, and Mick's been on edge. When I try asking him about it, figuring he'll feel better if he talks about what's bothering him, he shuts down like a department store on a Sunday night. "I don't want to talk about it, Iris," he says, and his dark eyes narrow as if he thinks I'm somehow part of the problem.

"I guess I'll make an omelette," Mick says. He doesn't sound like he wants to.

"That'd be great." I'm starting to like cooking—especially for Mick—but I don't always feel like it. "I'm kind of stressed about the college applications. I need to get it all done by next week. Katie's already finished."

"Katie's an idiot."

I know Mick's saying that because I told him how all Katie cares about is doing makeup and going clubbing. I've decided it's okay if I complain about Katie but not okay when Mick does it. It's one more thing I don't say. I could keep a list of all the things I've stopped saying around Mick. That list would be longer than the pros and cons I was working on before.

Mick's in the kitchen. I watch him crack six eggs into a plastic bowl, then whisk them together. I love his shoulders. He must feel me admiring him because he pauses as if he's posing for a photo.

"I hate making big decisions."

Mick turns away from the egg bowl. "It's clear to me what you should do."

"It is?" For the first time all afternoon, I feel my body begin to relax.

"Absolutely." I love the certainty in Mick's voice. If only I could be more like him. Confident, certain about things, in charge of my own life. Strong. "You should go to that private college you've been talking about. In Creative Arts."

"Ms. Odette thinks I should be an accountant."

"Ms. Odette should have her head examined."

I laugh when Mick says that.

"If you're determined, Joey, and if you put in the time to hone your craft—really hone it—then I know you'll make it as an actor. In fact, I guarantee it."

"You do?" I know Mick can't really guarantee I'll make it as an actor, but I also know he's right about being determined and putting in the time to hone my craft. I'm so lucky I've got him to talk to. And that he believes in me. I don't know how I'd manage without him. But I don't want to think about that. I don't ever plan—not ever—to be without Mick.

I recycle the other brochures, keeping only the one for the private college and the Creative Arts program. I'll fill out the application form after we have Mick's omelette. The whole apartment smells delicious.

I feel as light as a fairy in one of Shakespeare's comedies. My decision is made. So what if I didn't make it myself?

CHAPTER 18

"He took me by the wrist and held me hard..."
—HAMLET, ACT 2, SCENE 1

Most days after school, I go to the loft. If Mick's not at a meeting, we get a couple of hours together. Weeknights, I sleep at home. If I didn't, Mom would get suspicious. My single bed feels sad and small.

All week I look forward to Saturday. We spend all day together and at night we fall asleep, our legs tangled together, William Shakespeare curled around my head like an orange fur hat.

When I let myself in this Saturday morning, Mick is on the phone. I can tell from the clipped way he's speaking that he's talking to his lawyer. "That's ridiculous," Mick says, scowling into the phone. "I'll never give her that. Never. No way."

When I wave at Mick, he doesn't bother waving back. It's as if he hasn't even noticed me come in. William Shakespeare must be hiding. The cat is as sensitive to Mick's moods as I am.

Mrs. Karpman is in Toronto. I take her key from the kitchen drawer where I left it for safekeeping. At least Sunshine will be glad to see me.

The canary chirps when I come in. I change his water and add seed to the plastic dispenser. Even though Mrs. Karpman said I didn't need to change the wax paper at the bottom of his cage, I do it anyhow, sprinkling the fresh paper with gravel. When I do, Sunshine swoops down to the bottom of the cage as if to show me he's grateful that it's so nice and clean.

I've never seen so many knickknacks as in Mrs. Karpman's apartment. It turns out she doesn't only collect porcelain teacups and salt and pepper shakers. She's also got a shelf full of thimbles and two shelves of eggcups. Who ever heard of an eggcup collection? If she ever did move to Toronto, she'd need an extra moving van for her collections.

But though the apartment is crowded with her stuff and smells of mothballs, there's something surprisingly peaceful about being here. Maybe it's Sunshine's chirping or maybe it's the spirit of Mr. Karpman, but when I sit down in Mrs. Karpman's velvet armchair, I relax in a way I can't seem to relax at home or even at Mick's.

When I think of Mick, and as if on cue, I hear his voice booming through Mrs. Karpman's wall. "No way!" he's saying, and then I hear a thud. My shoulders stiffen. I hope Mick has just banged down the phone and not punched another hole in the wall. And I hope William Shakespeare isn't freaking out.

I don't want to go back to Mick's straightaway. I should give him time to cool off, calm down after the conversation with the lawyer, but the thought of William Shakespeare, who startles when he hears a loud noise, makes me go back a little sooner than I want to.

I wish Mick didn't have such an explosive temper. That's the right word for it: *explosive*. And it's hard to know what'll set him off. I know it comes with being passionate and creative. Mick gets upset because he cares so much— too much, maybe. I could never be with someone who wasn't passionate and creative or who didn't care too much. Even if that someone never lost his temper or raised his voice or put his fist through a wall. I know I'd be bored to death with anyone but Mick.

I let myself back into the loft as quietly as I can. I'll just check on William Shakespeare. Maybe I'll make some tea. Mick likes tea in the morning. He says it's bracing—whatever that means. Two spoons of sugar, no milk. I drink mine that way now too.

At first, there's no sign of William Shakespeare. I think of calling out for him, but even that might upset Mick if he's still angry.

Then I catch sight of William Shakespeare's orange tail. He has crawled under the bed, but he seems to be considering coming out now that I'm back. "Hey, William Shakespeare," I say under my breath, and a small paw emerges.

Mick is at the table, tapping furiously at his laptop.

"Sorry," I say.

"What are you sorry for this time?" he asks, without looking up.

"I'm sorry things are going badly with the lawyer. I'm sorry you're upset."

"That lawyer is an asshole. I hired him to work for me, not *her*." The angry way he says *her* makes me feel a little better. Sometimes, when I'm in my own bed at home, I worry that Mick might get back together with Nial's mother, for Nial's sake. But Mick could never go back to someone he hates so much. So passionately.

"How about a cup of tea? Two spoons of sugar, no milk." My voice rises on the word *milk*. I sound like some lady on a TV commercial for margarine or paper towels! It's because I want to fix Mick's mood, but I don't know how.

It's a crisp, sunny February day. The cold spell we've had all week has broken. With the temperature hovering around zero, it's a perfect day for a walk on the mountain or maybe a drive to the Laurentians. There, Mick and I wouldn't have to worry about running into anyone we know. We could just be ourselves and not have to hide who we are to each other. But now isn't a good time to

mention going for a walk or driving to the country. I reach
for the teapot. Even though Mick hasn't said he wants tea.

"Don't talk to me as if I'm a child." When Mick says
this—out of the blue—I'm so surprised I nearly drop the
teapot.

My mistake is talking back to Mick. I should've waited
for his black mood to pass. For the sky inside his head to
turn blue again. "I wasn't talking to you like a child. I only
asked if you wanted a cup of tea. I thought it would help
calm you down."

"Calm me down?! You think a bloody cup of tea with
two sugars and no milk"—Mick is imitating me now, the
way I sang out the words before, and the imitation is so
good, it makes me cringe—"will calm me down?! You
have no idea what I'm going through. No idea at all!"

"I do. I swear I do."

I've just stepped on a land mine.

Without thinking, I raise my elbow so it covers my face.

"What do you think I'm going to do, hit you, Iris?
Is that it?"

Oh no, I think. I've made things even worse by covering
my face. Why am I such an idiot?

"No, I don't think that," I say, and I realize I am cowering
too, like William Shakespeare under the bed. I don't know
what to do to get Mick to calm down. I don't know where
to go to get away from his anger. I have nowhere to go.

What happens next happens so quickly it's hard for me to keep track of what is going on. To process it. Mick grabs the neck of my T-shirt. "Let go," I say. "You're hurting me!"

Mick is so angry he's sputtering. All the while I'm thinking he isn't really angry with me. I haven't done anything wrong. Just offered him a cup of tea. If only I hadn't shielded my face with my elbow. I insulted him by doing that. So I let my elbow drop back down. I do it slowly, so Mick will notice. "Calm down, Mick. Please, calm down," I say, my voice starting to break. "Please!"

Mick's eyes are cold as marbles. I watch his fist coming through the air like a baseball. This time, there's no wall behind me. I try ducking, but I'm not fast enough. Again, I get the weird feeling that part of me is watching from a distance. That I'm both the actor and the audience. That my mind manages to duck in time but not my body—and my mind is somewhere up near the ceiling, watching the terrible scene unfolding below.

Mick punches my right cheek. The pain is so sudden and intense, I crumple to the floor, doubled over. The inside of my head is ringing. How, the part of me watching from a distance wonders, can flesh ring?

"You had it coming, Iris." His voice is coming from far away. Why isn't he calling me *Joey* the way he always does?

Besides the terrible pain in my cheek all the way up to my right eye, I only know one thing: Mick sounds calmer now. Much calmer. Like himself again. And despite the pain, I'm glad the storm is over.

CHAPTER 19

"...I could be bounded in a nutshell and count myself a king of infinite space, were it not that I have bad dreams."
—*HAMLET*, ACT 2, SCENE 2

I don't expect Mick to apologize. He doesn't believe in apologies, the way other people don't believe in Santa Claus or the tooth fairy. I haven't heard him apologize to the lawyer after he's yelled at him on the phone, and I'll bet anything he's never apologized to Nial's mother either. Not apologizing is a point of pride for Mick.

Personally, I don't see the problem with apologizing. I apologized to Katie for missing her party. I apologized to Mom for being too busy to meet up for regular Saturday brunches at the bagel place. I even apologize to strangers when I'm trying to pass them on the escalator in the metro and our elbows bump. Apologizing makes me feel better, not worse. If anything, I probably apologize too *much*.

Even though I'm the one with the bruised cheek and eye, I actually feel sorry for Mick. He has to look at me this way, and every time he does, he has to remember how he lost it and ended up hurting me. That must kill him. Even if he won't say so. I know it would kill me.

I tried icing my face right after the incident—I used a bag of peas from Mick's freezer—but it didn't help much. Later, I couldn't sleep on my right side the way I like to.

When I got up this morning, I went straight to the bathroom to inspect my face. It was as if I'd somehow expected the swelling to magically go down, maybe even disappear altogether. Only of course it hadn't. And now there's bruising too. It breaks my heart to look at my mangled face. The skin around my eye's the worst, probably because it's so thin. It's as purple as a ripe eggplant, and it hurts when I blink. I feel ugly—not just outside, but inside too. If only I hadn't been so stupid. So what if I make the honor roll? I'm starting to think I need to be in a remedial section of life!

I call in sick to Scoops. Phil says not to worry; he'll find a replacement. "You sure you're okay, Iris?" he asks.

I cover the side of my face when Phil asks me that. There I go being stupid again. It isn't as if he can see me.

I won't be able to leave the loft all day, that's for sure. I don't even want to think about Monday. I'll have to come up with some excuse when people at school ask what happened. Because this time, they're definitely going to ask.

I also need to figure out what to tell Mom. That's when my eyes land on Mick's kitchen cabinets. Perfect. I'll say I bumped into a cabinet door. That I didn't realize it was open. That I can be such a klutz sometimes. I'll need to put my acting skills to good use. I'll demonstrate what happened. I'll throw my head back to show how startled I was. "I know it looks awful," I'll say, and then I'll laugh lightheartedly. "People'll think someone hit me! Can you imagine that? Someone hitting me?"

"How do you want to spend the day, Joey?" Mick asks me over Sunday breakfast. He must've heard me talking to Phil. Mick has made poached eggs—I know it's his way of trying to make up for last night. What's weird is how when he looks at me Mick doesn't seem to notice my swollen cheek and eye. Maybe, I think hopefully, it's not really that bad. Maybe I'm making too much of it, overreacting. If Mick doesn't notice…except then I lift my knife and catch my reflection in it. I'm so ugly I have to put the knife down. I want to cry and never stop, but I know I can't cry in front of Mick. I don't want him to think I'm weak or to know I'm feeling sorry for myself.

"I just want to stay in," I manage to tell him, but then I realize maybe that'll make him feel guilty so I add, "I need to finish off that college application."

"Sounds like a plan. Let's make it a day for organizing—and lying low." Mick doesn't say it in a way that suggests

I've got a reason to lie low. It's more like we've been busy and we need to catch up on chores around the loft. "I've got a lot of computer work to do," he adds.

I'm going to be gentle with myself today. Someone has to be. I take my time finalizing the application, reviewing every line, and then, after making sure no one's in the corridor, I go to Mrs. Karpman's to feed Sunshine. I sit in Mrs. Karpman's armchair, surrounded by the photographs of all her children and grandchildren. I can't remember the eldest grandson's name, but Mrs. Karpman's right—he is good-looking. In a boyish way. Something about his face—the openness, maybe—reminds me of his grandfather. No wonder Mrs. Karpman's so crazy about him.

When I get back to Mick's, he is busy on his laptop. I don't ask whether he's heard from the lawyer or if he's writing an email to him now. There's no way I'm going to step on that land mine again.

I wander back to the bathroom, where I hoist myself onto the edge of the sink and really look at myself in the mirror. I start with my left side, then turn my head slowly. I've always liked my profile, the way my nose goes up a little at the bottom, but not too much. My lips are nice too, even without lip gloss. They have a nice bow shape.

Mom says that when I was a baby, she used to stand over my crib and admire my lips. Was my father with her when she did that? Were things already bad between them?

Maybe next time I talk to my dad, or if he comes back to Plattsburgh, I could ask him.

Slowly I turn my head so that I can see the right side of my face. I wince when I do. It looks like it belongs to a monster.

Part of me still wants to cry, but Mick would hear, and I don't want that. Besides, crying won't do me any good. My salty tears might make things worse, might make the skin look even puffier.

I let the cold water run until it's so cold it makes my fingers ache. Then I take a small square washcloth from the towel rack and hold it under the water. I squeeze it out and fold it in two so it makes a compress. I sit down on the toilet and hold the compress to the right side of my face. I'm careful not to press too hard. The skin is so sensitive.

I take a deep breath. Maybe the cold compress will help bring down the swelling. And I'm pretty sure I saw some Vitamin-E oil in Mick's bathroom cabinet. When I get up, I'll look for it. I read somewhere that Vitamin E speeds up healing. I need Vitamin E all over everywhere.

After I find the Vitamin E and dab a little on with just one fingertip, I suddenly feel very, very tired. More tired, even, than I've felt on the nights I used to go clubbing with Katie. Or even after a double shift at Scoops. I need to lie down.

"I'm going to take a little nap," I tell Mick.

He doesn't look up from the computer. "Good idea."

I lie down on the bed, and it isn't long before I feel myself falling into a half-doze. Resting will help me heal; I know it will. The sun is streaming into the room, but when I close my eyes (it hurts a little when I close them), I'm in a deep, dark forest. The trees are so tall that even when I tilt my head, I can't see all the way to the top. When I look back down at the ground, there's no path for me to follow. The trees are so dense that hardly any light can get in. How will I ever find my way out of here?

From somewhere a world away, I hear a gentle clattering. Has someone come to rescue me—to lead me out of the forest? Then I realize I'm half-asleep in Mick's loft. He's gotten up to close the curtains so I'll be able to sleep better. I smile because Mick is looking after me. Smiling hurts my face. Then I hear Mick mutter something about how the sun is in his eyes and he's having trouble reading what's on the computer screen.

I go back and forth between the apartment and the forest. The forest floor sinks under my feet when I try to take a step forward. What if I sink too? Who'll find me here? No one will know where I am. And no one is coming to save me. I need to save myself. But how, when I'm afraid to even take a step?

Where did all these leaves come from? They are covering me so softly that I'm less afraid. I feel my lips curl into a small smile. Oh, that feels nice and warm.

It's Mick. He's covering me with the comforter, tucking it in around my hips and over my feet so I won't get cold. See, I think, he is looking after me. This time I don't smile though.

I know Mick loves me. Adores me. And I know he's sorry for what he's done. So what if he can't say so in words?

I have to spend the night at Mick's. Mom would freak out if she saw me looking like this. I phone to tell her I'll be at school rehearsing until late, and that it makes more sense to sleep over at Katie's since her house is closer to the school than ours.

Mom says she's worried I'm spending so much time in rehearsal. "You sound exhausted, Iris. Can we at least plan a quiet evening at home tomorrow? It would be good for both of us. I've been putting in long hours at work too," she says. "I'll make us a batch of chicken wings." Chicken wings were my favorite when I was six. I don't tell her that now I think they're greasy and too much effort for too little chicken.

"I'll try," I say instead.

Should I mention I bumped into a cabinet? Prepare her for when she sees me? In the end, I decide not to.

Who knows? Maybe by tomorrow night my face'll be back to normal.

At the end of the afternoon, I check my Facebook page. My father has messaged me. *Fingers crossed*, he writes, *that this deal is going to work. This one really feels big. We're on the cusp of something major here. Will keep you posted. Say hello to Ophelia. Love, Dad.*

I'm still his only Facebook friend. That pleases me, because it confirms he only got on to Facebook so he could find me.

I read his message over. He didn't ask how I am.

In a way, I'm glad. I'd have had to lie to him too.

～

Katie would know what to do about my face. Part of me wishes I could tell her what happened and ask for her help. But she'd never understand.

Katie isn't too impressed by my regular makeup routine, which never takes me more than five minutes max. "What kind of actress doesn't care about makeup?" she asked me after rehearsal last week.

"This kind," I told her. "And the preferred word these days is *actor*, not *actress*."

"You could do a lot more with yourself, Iris. Really, you could. If only you put in a little effort. And used mascara."

"I hate mascara. It leaves tire tracks on your cheeks."

"Lenore's using this new product that makes your eyelashes grow. It costs a hundred and sixty bucks a bottle. But you should see her eyelashes. They're amazing."

"It sounds like you and Lenore are getting pretty tight."

"Lenore makes time for her friends," Katie said. "Unlike some people I know."

On a regular day, I put on a little eye shadow—pink over the lid, grey in the crease—and a touch of clear lip gloss. Concealer when I have a zit. But this morning I spend thirty-five minutes on makeup. I can't help thinking Katie would be impressed.

I use half a tube of concealer. It says *Let the real you shine through* in white letters on the outside of the tube. The real me? I'm not sure who that is anymore. Then again, I'm not sure I ever knew. I'll need to buy more concealer after school. Using just the tips of my fingers—the skin still feels tender to the touch—I apply the gooey cream all over my face, putting an extra layer on the right side. There's still some swelling, but at least I've got the color almost right.

The bigger job is making my eyelids match. The purple in my eye shadow compact isn't dark enough, so I mix in some gray. And I use a little yellow at the corner, under the crease. Yes, that's good.

The upside of focusing so much on getting the colors right is there isn't time to feel sorry for myself. That only happens afterward, when I'm pushing open the door to Westwood.

I take a deep breath. *It's just another performance, Iris,* I tell myself. *You can do it. Break a leg.*

The noise hits me like a too-strong smell. Lockers slamming shut, swearing, laughter, the secretary's voice on the PA system saying someone's forgotten to turn off the lights on a green Toyota parked in the school lot. Is it always so noisy or am I extra sensitive after hiding out in the loft all weekend?

Though Tommy's the last person on earth I want to see right now, he practically crashes into me. Someone should tell him it isn't wise to jog down the school corridors. I throw my hands up. I don't think I can handle another ounce of pain. "Hey, Iris," he says, blushing when he sees it's me, "what's up?" Is he looking at me funny or am I imagining it?

"Not much," I say. I won't mention the kitchen cabinet "accident" unless I have to.

I'm worried he'll say he misses me or that he wants to talk. What'll I say then? But when he doesn't say either of those things, somehow I feel a little disappointed. Now I can feel Tommy's eyes on my face. "If you don't mind my saying, Iris, you look a little...off. You didn't meet some guy in a dark alley, did you?"

I laugh lightheartedly, just the way I practiced in my head. Here goes, I think, it's time for me to try out my story. This can be my audition. "I walked right into one of our kitchen cabinets—can you believe I didn't realize it was open? *Bang!* This happened. I'm such a klutz. Tell me the truth—do I look totally gross?"

"You could never look gross."

I pat Tommy's arm. "Hey, thanks."

I want to get away, but Tommy won't let me. "You're not hanging out with that friend of Ms. Cameron's, are you?"

"Of course not." I roll my eyes to show him he doesn't know what he's talking about.

"It's just…that Jeep I saw you in. It's his, isn't it?"

I'm feeling cornered. "He gave me a lift once," I tell Tommy. "It was no big deal. Remember how snowy it was outside that day? He saw me waiting at the bus."

"You had the cat with you…" I can feel Tommy trying to figure things out.

"Forget it, will you?"

"You sure you're okay?" Tommy's forehead is scrunched up like some old man's.

"I'm sure."

"Antoine said he thought he saw you—"

I don't let Tommy finish his sentence. "He didn't."

Katie finds me at my locker. "What's with the purple and yellow eye makeup, Iris? You look like a crack whore."

Katie laughs. I laugh too. Even more lightheartedly than before. "I had a little incident—with a kitchen cabinet. One eye got kinda bruised."

Katie winces. "That must've hurt."

"It was more the humiliation than anything else. I mean, can you imagine being so ditzy? I didn't even realize the cabinet door was wide-open. Anyway, you know how you're always telling me to put more effort into my makeup? Well, that's what I did this morning. I was hoping you'd be impressed."

"Effort is good," Katie says, tilting her head to get a better look at my eyes. "But I'd say go for a more subtle effect. If I were you, I'd ease off on all that yellow. It doesn't work with your complexion."

CHAPTER 20

"...break, my heart, for I must hold my tongue."
—*HAMLET*, ACT 1, SCENE 2

It's a long time before my face looks completely normal again. I try not to think about what happened and how Mick lost it, but little things remind me—like the washcloth hanging on the towel rack in his bathroom.

I wish I wasn't so influenced by Mick's moods. When he's in a dark mood, the thunderclouds roll in on me too. My shoulders tense up and my stomach rumbles like it knows trouble's on the way.

When he's in a great mood, like he is today, I catch it too. Everything makes me laugh. My spirit is so light I feel like if I stretched out my arms and took a leap, I could fly.

I guess when you love someone as much as I love Mick, you feel everything he does. Sometimes I wonder if I'm more tuned in to Mick's feelings than to my own. Is it like this for everyone who's in love? Maybe some people are better at keeping a part of themselves just for themselves, but that isn't how love works for me. I can't hold any part of myself back. Not from Mick. Besides, I wouldn't want to.

He wants to take me shopping downtown. I already know we're going to have a blast!

We traipse in and out of the little boutiques along Saint Catherine Street—the souvenir stores, the shops that carry buttery leather jackets, a cigar store—ending up at a department store, where Mick needs to buy socks. Mick forgets *not* to hold my hand, and when he does, I don't say anything. I just hold his, aware of the delicious sensation of his long cool fingers laced through mine. How nuts am I for this guy that just holding hands gets me hot?

After we buy the socks, Mick suggests we go down the street to Forever 21. Inside the store, we stand so close on the escalator that I can feel him breathing into my hair. A woman on the down escalator wrinkles her nose when she passes us. Mick and I both crack up. I catch our reflection in the mirrored wall next to the escalator. Mick has slid his knee between my legs. We look so great together. So happy. So sexy. If only there were some way to make this moment last forever. Of course, I know it's a silly thought. Who'd want to spend eternity on an escalator? Maybe me—if I knew I'd be with Mick and he'd always be in the mood he's in today.

The music's blaring on the second floor. Rihanna is wailing: *"When the sun shines, we'll shine together. Told you I'll be here forever."* I wriggle to the beat.

"Why don't you try this on?" Mick says, raising his voice so I'll hear him over Rihanna. He's picked out a very short red plaid skirt for me.

"I don't know." I want to say the skirt isn't really me, but I don't want to disappoint him.

So I say I'll try it on. He picks a low-cut red T-shirt to go with it. I notice a black linen shirtdress that's more my style. It has red heart-shaped buttons down the front. "What do you think?" I ask Mick.

"I can't tell," he says. When he grins, I can tell he's planning another wild surprise. "You'll have to try it on."

There's a girl my age supervising the dressing rooms. She has a bored expression on her face.

"You wait for me here," I tell Mick. "I'll come out and model for you."

"I've got three items," I tell the salesgirl. She gives me a robotic smile and hands me a miniature hanger with the number three on it. When I turn around, I expect to see Mick sitting on one of the chairs by the dressing rooms, but he's disappeared. He doesn't answer when I call for him. "Mick!" I try again. "I'm just going to try the stuff on! Meet me out here, okay?"

I go into the dressing room and slip off my T-shirt and jeans and socks. I'm hanging my clothes on a hook behind the door when it opens just a sliver. I'm about to call out—maybe it's another customer who thinks this room is empty—when I spot Mick's fedora and his tousled hair underneath. Every time I see him, I'm struck all over again by how handsome he is.

"You shouldn't be in here," I whisper, but I'm giggling as I say it. Mick has a pile of clothing draped over one arm. A maxi dress, more T-shirts, the same plaid skirt in another color.

He tosses the clothes onto the chair at the back of the dressing room. I can feel him checking me out—I'm down to just my bra and undies. His eyes are moving up and down my body so slowly it's as if he's touching me.

Mick backs up against the wall. Before he even loosens his belt, I know what he wants to do. He's totally crazy!

"Mick, we can't," I whisper, but my voice is rough and I know I don't sound as if I mean it, even to my own ears.

"I want you, Joey," Mick whispers into my ear. "Right here. Right now." He reaches into his back pocket to show me he's brought a condom. Then he pulls down his jeans.

"What if someone hears?"

Mick is already pulling off my undies. He uses the weight of his body to push me up against the side wall of the dressing room. I could say no, but I don't. I want this too. At least, I think I do. I help him slide on the condom.

"Everything okay in there?" the salesgirl calls. Thank God she doesn't sound suspicious. Mick must have snuck by her when she was busy folding clothes or putting them back on the racks.

"Just fine," I manage to say.

I love to watch Mick's face when we make love. Just before he comes, he closes his eyes, and he looks totally peaceful. As if nothing in the world—not lawyers, not actors who don't know their parts, not even the stupid things I sometimes say—could ever bother him. All the little lines on his face disappear—the ones across his forehead and near his eyes, and the really tiny ones over his lips—and then he makes this throaty groan and calls out *Joey*, and I feel so happy, so proud. Of all the women in the world, I'm the one Mick wants. I'm the only one who can make him feel like this.

If I wasn't so stressed out about the salesgirl hearing us, I know I'd have come too. It hasn't happened yet, but I know it will. I also know it won't help if I think too much about it. I know I just need to relax and let it happen.

"*Told you I'll be here forever.*" I don't mean to say the line out loud.

"What's that?" Mick asks as he zips up his fly.

"I can't get that song off my brain."

Mick likes every single thing I try on. He gives me a thumbs-up for the red plaid kilt and the red T-shirt he picked to go with it. I prefer the shirtdress—I could wear it to school with leggings. Mick thinks it's okay, though he isn't crazy about the buttons. He really likes the maxi dress, the other T-shirts and the plaid kilt in blue.

"But I can't get everything," I tell him. "It'd be way too expensive." Mick hasn't said he'll pay, but I know he's going to offer. I also know he needs to watch his spending. The lawyer charges for every minute on the phone. The last thing I want is for Mick to end up in debt the way I think my father must have. "I'll just take the plaid skirt," I tell him. "It's your favorite, right?"

"You're getting all of it, and it won't be expensive at all." Mick winks, but I don't get the joke.

"Of course it'll be expensive." I'm checking the price tag on the maxi dress. "This one's sixty dollars."

"You must've missed the sign, Joey. All this stuff's on sale!" Mick says, gathering up the dress, the blue kilt and the other T-shirts he brought into the dressing room.

"The sign?" What is Mick talking about? "I don't want you buying them for me." I don't mention the lawyer or Nial or my father. I'm afraid to break the spell of this perfect afternoon.

"We'll pay for this," Mick whispers, handing me the red kilt and T-shirt. "I'm not so sure about this," he says, handing me the shirtdress. "We'll tell her you don't want that." I nearly tell Mick that I do want that dress—that I like it more than any of the other things I tried on—but I figure it's not worth arguing about.

Nothing could prepare me for what happens next.

Mick fishes an army knife out of the front pocket of his jeans. I never even knew he carried an army knife. Then he fiddles with the security tag on the maxi dress. "What are you doing?" I ask.

"Having some fun." He uses the blade to snip the plastic tag, then the screwdriver attachment to pry the pin inside loose. He's careful to catch the pin before it falls to the floor. Then he folds the dress, along with all the other clothes he brought in with him—and puts them into the main compartment of my backpack.

I shake my head. "You can't do that," I whisper. "It's stealing."

"Bah," Mick says. "It's not called stealing when you take it from a corporation as large as Forever 21. It's called justice. Companies like this gouge consumers. That sixty-dollar skirt probably cost them a few pennies. It's got hardly any fabric. Besides, this is an adventure, Joey."

I don't tell Mick about the sick feeling in my stomach. "We could get arrested," I say instead.

Mick holds my hand the whole time he's paying for the two items. He also keeps up a steady conversation with the salesgirl. "We weren't sure about that shirtdress," he tells her. "The buttons are a little odd. What do you think of the buttons? Be honest, all right?"

"I hope you found everything you wanted," the sales-girl says when she hands me my shopping bag. I hope she doesn't notice I'm trembling. "You two have a great day now."

We take the escalator back down to the main floor. This time, I don't look at our reflection in the mirror. All I can think about is that there must be security guards everywhere—some dressed like ordinary shoppers. Are they on to us? I'm afraid to make eye contact with anyone. Afraid they'll read the guilt in my face.

I don't even let myself breathe till we're out of the store and halfway down the block.

Mick is tugging on my arm, steering me toward Peel Street, where we've parked the Jeep.

It's only when I'm sitting in the Jeep and Mick is turning on the motor that I realize my mistake.

I was wrong to say, *We could get arrested.*

I was the one who could've been arrested.

Not Mick.

CHAPTER 21

"O vengeance!
Why, what an ass am I!" —HAMLET, ACT 2, SCENE 2

I hate it when I can't find something. Especially when it's something important like my college application. I know I put it in a brown envelope, but where is it? At first, I think it'll turn up somewhere obvious. Under the pile of scripts and newspapers by Mick's sofa. On the counter in his kitchen, where he keeps the mail. But I can't find the brown envelope anywhere. Which is when I start to panic.

"Shit! Shit! Shit!" I never swear, so the words feel weird in my mouth. Rather than making me feel better, which Katie says swearing does for her, it only makes me feel worse. More stressed. I go through the pile of scripts and newspapers again. What if Mick put it in the green recycling box? Then what?

I can't find the envelope anywhere.

"Shit!"

I can't phone Mick. He's in a meeting with some theater people from Quebec City who've come to talk to him about a theater festival they're organizing this summer. "This is a major opportunity for me, Joey," he told me last night. "For both of us."

So I text Mick. cant find colg app. U seen it? Brn evlp. Strssd. Luv U.

I hope he'll answer straightaway and tell me where the envelope is, but he doesn't. Looking at the blank screen on my cell phone makes me even more upset.

I pull open the kitchen drawer, though it doesn't make any sense to look in it. Who'd put an envelope where the cutlery goes? There's nothing there, of course, except forks and knives and spoons, all nestled in their separate compartments.

"Shit!"

I slam the drawer closed so hard that I bang my wrist. I rub the bone, and for a moment I see myself—rubbing my wrist in Mick's tiny kitchen.

Okay, Iris, I tell myself, *calm down. You're losing it.* And then I think, Is this what losing it feels like? Is this what happens to Mick when he gets so angry he explodes? So angry he can't stop himself? It must be like being on a train that's going too fast and flying off the track, only you're not a passenger—you're the train. I close my eyes to make the feeling stop.

I make myself sit down on the sofa and breathe. In and out, slowly, over and over again. When I can feel my whole body begin to relax, I let myself think about the envelope. But not in a panicky way this time. I need to keep my train on the track. Where was I the last time I saw it? I was right here. The envelope was on the coffee table. I'd just double-checked every line. Why didn't I put it right into my back-pack so it'd be there now? I stop myself again. There's no point in thinking that. *Go back to the coffee table, Iris. See it in your mind.* What happened next?

This time, the answer comes. Mick was doing some paperwork. I can picture him scooping up his papers and shuffling them so they'd be in a neat pile with their edges lined up. Mick's particular that way. Did he accidentally pick up my envelope? Maybe that's why I can't find it.

Mick keeps his personal papers—including the ones he was busy with that day—by his side of the bed. So I go over there now. Even from here, I can see there are several brown envelopes in his pile. Maybe mine's in there. My wrist throbs a little. Silly me to get so upset over nothing when all I had to do was replay the scene in my head.

My phone vibrates on the coffee table. It's probably Mick texting me back. I'll check the phone later. First, I want that envelope.

I find it right away. It's near the top of the pile. I recog-nize my own neat handwriting. *Iris Wagner.* My mom's return address underneath, of course. One day, maybe even by next year, I'll have the same address as Mick. That'll be as soon as I turn eighteen and we can stop hiding our relationship. By then, Mick's life will be more settled, so he'll be calmer. There'll be no more fights. I'm sure of it.

I don't know what makes me look at the other envelopes in the pile. I know Mick wouldn't like it. He's a very private person. But Mick isn't here to get upset with me. Besides, what harm is there in looking? I love Mick so much. I just want to know him even better so I can love him more, understand him better.

There's an envelope marked *Nial*. I've only seen that one photo of Mick's son, and I'm curious to see if there are more inside the envelope. I slide my hand into the envelope and pull out what's inside. No photos—just papers that look like legal documents. One with a red-and-gold seal catches my eye. I open it and see something about a restraining order. What is a *restraining order* exactly—and why is there one in the Nial envelope? I skim the words on the page.

Which is when I learn that last July—exactly two months before I met Mick—the Commonwealth of Australia issued a restraining order against him. According to this document, Mick is not allowed to go within twenty-five meters of Millicent Temple, who must be his ex-wife, Nial's mother. It also says he's not allowed to contact her by telephone or email and that his visits with his son Nial have to be supervised by a state-approved social worker.

My hands shake as I read. I think I know why Mick is not allowed within twenty-five meters of Millicent Temple. But why would she insist that someone be there to supervise Mick's visits with his son? It doesn't make any sense.

There's another envelope, marked *Millicent*. This one seems to have quite a bit of stuff inside and the seal looks worn, as if the envelope's been opened and closed many times.

I fish the envelope out of the pile. A photograph falls out. It's of Nial and a woman who must be Millicent. I can tell right away she's Nial's mom. They have the same fair hair and laughing expression. I tremble a little as I inspect the photograph. Millicent is younger than I expected. She's probably around twenty, just a few years older than me.

I reach into the envelope to see what else is there. A menu from a fish restaurant in Melbourne. Tickets to a show. More tickets. And then a crumpled piece of lined paper with a poem on it. I only need to read a few lines.

Until you.
I was small and lost, like a rudderless ship.
Until you.
Nothing made sense.

My poem. The one he wrote for me. Only he didn't. This poem is dated three years ago. He wrote it for her. For Millicent.

I rush to the bathroom and get there just in time to vomit into the sink.

~

The very worst part is having no one to talk to. Not Katie, not my mom, not even Mrs. Karpman, who's still away in Toronto. So I keep up a running conversation in my head.

The restraining order is no big deal. Millicent is a difficult person. That's obvious from the way Mick talks about her. And I remember too that Mick once said Nial's mother knows a lot of lawyers. He said her uncle is a lawyer in Melbourne. I'll bet she got that restraining order just to get on Mick's case, to make him look bad, and to get even with him for breaking off their relationship. And the business about the supervised visits—well, it's the dumbest thing I ever heard. Millicent shouldn't be interfering in Mick's relationship with his son. Nobody knows that better than I do. Besides, Mick is crazy about Nial. He'd never do anything to hurt that little boy.

Or would he?

The poem is no big deal either.

Oh yes, it is a big deal. He made you think it was just for you. That you were special. He deceived you.

Maybe he used the same poem because he was blocked—you know, artistically. Because of the legal stuff. The poor guy's been under so much pressure. I'll only add to the pressure if I mention the restraining order. Or the poem.

Plus, he won't like that you've been going through his papers.

That might set him off. And you don't want that, do you, Iris?

The vibrating movement of my cell phone interrupts the conversation I've got going in my head. Thank God it's not Mick. I don't know what I'd say to him right now.

It's Phil. "Listen, Iris. I don't like to bug you during the week. I know you're tied up with school and that play of yours. Shakespeare, right? He sure was some genius. And plays, well, they're the greatest. Way better than tv. Anyway, Iris, the reason I'm calling is Suzanne phoned in sick and I'm wondering could you help me out here and do an evening shift? You'd be done by eleven. The tips are way better at night, Iris. People are more relaxed. They're out having a good time. People need to get out—"

I say yes—not just because I want to get Phil off the phone, and not just because of the bigger tips.

It's mostly because I don't know what else to do with myself. I'll leave a note for Mick to tell him where I've gone. I don't want him to worry.

There's a thick line of customers waiting to get into Scoops. It's only March, but maybe ice cream on a Saturday night makes people think they're getting a head start on spring. Anyway, I'm glad the restaurant is busy. I won't have time to think about Mick and those papers.

Phil raises one hand when he sees me, spreading his fingers. He's telling me he needs me on the floor in five minutes. Thank God, I think, that he's too busy to talk. I rush to the back bathroom to change into the dreaded uniform. My nurse's shoes smell of leather and sour ice cream. The white laces have gone gray.

There's bad news—the busboy has also called in sick. "We need to pick up the dirty dishes ourselves," Joyce, the other waitress, tells me when I'm grabbing my pen and order pad. "And we're outta soda spoons. I'm getting too old for this lousy job. At least you've got a future, kid. This is my life."

Why is it that everyone wants an ice-cream soda when we're out of soda spoons? Between orders, I gather a dozen or so of the long spoons from the big gray tubs we use for collecting dirty dishes and scramble to the kitchen at the back of the restaurant. As I run the spoons under hot water, soaping them with an old sponge, Chen, the dishwasher, scowls. "I'm doing the best I can here," he growls.

There's no point serving an ice-cream soda with a short spoon. You need a soda spoon to get to the ice cream and the syrup at the bottom—which are the best parts. And without the right spoons, my tips are going to suffer.

A tall man with dark hair sits down at the counter. For a second, I remember when Mick sat in the same spot. That was our beginning. When everything was possible. Before anything bad had happened. The place where our story began.

"Excuse me, miss, but can you take our order, please? We've been waiting forever—and then some," someone calls from a booth by the wall.

"Sorry about that," I say as I pour water. "Crazy night here. What can I get you folks?"

"Hey, Iris!" a girl's voice calls from somewhere in the lineup to get in. Even before I turn around, I know who it is. Lenore. I wave—and hope to God she won't end up in my section. But God must be busy with other people's problems, because a second later Lenore calls out, "We really want you to be our waitress!" You have to know Lenore well—the way I do—to know she's said it in a mean way.

I flip my order pad to a fresh page as I approach their table. It takes everything I have to be nice to Lenore and the three guys she's with—trust her to be out with three guys, though one's a cousin. "She's Ophelia in the play," Lenore tells the cousin. "It's not as big a role as mine, of course, but still, it's a start. You know, Iris," she says, looking back at me, "that uniform looks supercute on you. I love the puffed sleeves."

"Thanks, Lenore," I say, wishing I could slug her. "So have you guys decided what you want?"

I get their order as quickly as I can. But as I'm heading back to the kitchen, I hear Lenore whispering—in one of those nasty, too-loud whispers that's meant to be overheard. "Poor thing has to work. Her mom cleans closets. I heard the dad was some kind of scammer."

How dare she talk about me like that? My mom runs her own business, and how would Lenore know anything about my father? Now I really want to slug that bitch. But I know I can't, so I grit my teeth and force myself to keep moving.

Three customers are getting up to leave, and I've got to clear their table before the next ones sit down. I can feel the checkered fabric under my arms getting damp. Can anger make a person sweat?

I sweep the dishes off the table and dump them in the gray tub on top of one of the trolleys. I still need a clean dishrag to mop the table, which is all sticky.

Shoot! I've nearly forgotten about a customer sitting alone at one of my booths. I'm about to go take his order when I see him snap his fingers at me. For a second I think I've imagined it, but the hard clicking sound carries in the air.

He's treating me like some dog he's calling to attention. Even Lenore turns to see what's going on.

There's no way on earth I'm going to apologize to this douchebag for not getting his order quickly enough. No way. How dare he snap his fingers at me! Who does he think he is? More important, who does he think I am?

My eyes land on the gray tub. If the busboy were here, he'd never have let it get so full. Soda spoons are sticking up out of the tub like masts in a crowded harbor. The glasses and cups inside are coated with a cloudy film of leftover ice cream. Balled-up napkins are stuffed wherever there's a bit of space. The only color comes from the half-chewed gumballs left over from some kid's scoop of bubblegum ice cream.

I suck in my breath when I pick up the tub. It's heavy and hard to carry because it's jammed so full. Leaning back a little on the heels of my nurse's shoes, I carry the tub, letting one end rest on my stomach, over to the man. The one who snapped his fingers.

"Yes," I say, smiling at him from behind the tub. "Can I help you?"

And then, just like that, as if it's the most natural thing in the world, I dump it on him. The spoons, the glasses and cups, the balled-up napkins and the half-chewed gumballs. They're on him, on his eyeglasses, on his shirt, on his table.

The guy jumps up from his seat, shaking the mess off him like a wet dog. His eyes look like they're about to pop out of his head. "What the hell!" he shouts. From somewhere far away, I hear Lenore's voice calling out, "Oh my god! Look what she did! She's crazy!"

Joyce comes running over with a pile of dry dishtowels.

Phil is coming now too. His lips are forming an angry *O*. I know he's going to fire me. And probably make a long speech about it too.

I hold my order pad in front of my chest like a shield. Before Phil can fire me or make a speech, I quit.

CHAPTER 22

"O limed soul, that, struggling to be free,
Art more engaged!" —HAMLET, ACT 3, SCENE 3

I 'm walking down Saint Catherine Street when I realize I'm still wearing the friggin' uniform. I cross my arms over my chest to hide the awful checkered blouse. Why didn't I change before I stomped out of there? Now I'll have to go back next week to get my clothes. Why am I such a complete and total idiot?

I phone Mick. We texted each other earlier and he said he'd pick me up at 11:15. But that's not for nearly two hours. I really need to talk to him, to tell him what happened and ask him to come get me right away. He'll say I was right to quit; he'll laugh when I tell him how I dumped the gray tub on that guy who snapped his fingers. But Mick's not picking up his phone. I try texting him again: Emrgcy. Quit job. Whr r u?

He must've turned off his phone again. Or let it run out of juice. What's the use of a cell phone if it's off half the time or you forget to keep it charged?

There's no way I'm waiting downtown. Not in this getup, that's for sure. At least I'll never have to wear it again after tonight. I'm going to burn these nurse's shoes. Picturing the shoes on fire cheers me up a little.

Where is Mick anyway? He said he'd be spending the night at the loft, that he had script notes to review. He's probably there now, working, too distracted to pick up his phone. Halfway down the block, I see the yellow light of a vacant cab coming my way. I rush to the curb and flag it down.

When I open the cab door, I'm nearly knocked over by a wave of lemony aftershave. Someone needs to tell this guy too much aftershave is bad for business. The change in my apron jingles when I take a deep breath and hop in. I give the cabbie Mick's address and try not to inhale. He looks at me in the rearview mirror but doesn't say a word. He can probably tell I've had a hard night.

When my arms get a little itchy, I don't think anything of it at first. I scratch the skin around my elbows, figuring the itchy feeling will pass.

Only it doesn't. I'm getting itchier. My legs, especially behind my knees, are getting crazy itchy, and so is my chest.

I bet I'm having an allergic reaction to this guy's after-shave. I lower my window and take a deep gulp of the night air. But I'm still itching like crazy. I scratch my legs so hard, I'm afraid I'll leave nail marks. I itch every-where—even the soles of my feet are itchy.

"I think I'm allergic to your aftershave," I tell the cabbie.

He opens the other windows. "I'm sorry for the after-shave," he says when we're finally at Mick's building and I'm reaching into my apron for the cab fare.

I turn to look at the cabbie when he says that. It feels like it's been forever since anyone apologized to me.

I hit the buzzer downstairs, but I don't wait for Mick to buzz me in. I need to get out of this uniform NOW. And I need Mick to hold me tight the way he does and tell me everything will be all right. Now and forever. Thank God for Mick. He knows how to make everything better.

It's only when I'm in the elevator, under fluores-cent lighting, that I notice the welts. Raised pinkish spots the size of mosquito bites, only more swollen and angry-looking. No wonder I'm so itchy. What are these things?

I fly down the hallway to Mick's apartment. "Mick!" I cry out, banging on the door. "Let me in!" I'm too stressed out to bother with the key. "Mick!"

There's no answer.

When I let myself in, it's obvious that except for William Shakespeare meowing by the door, no one's home.

That's weird. Mick said he'd be here.

I check my cell phone. Still no text message from Mick. But his phone's not charging at the wall by the couch the way I thought it might be. No, he has his phone with him.

I'm getting itchier.

It can't be the cabbie's lemon-scented aftershave. I look at my arms. There are even more pink welts than before. Hives. That's what these things must be. I've broken out in hives.

I need a hot bath NOW. With bubbles.

While the water's running, I do a quick search online about hives. The pictures on the screen confirm my diagnosis. Hives can be triggered by food allergies and sometimes by stress. Hot baths are not a good idea. Lukewarm ones are recommended. No bubbles. Oatmeal. *Oatmeal?* An antihistamine can help.

I add cold water to the tub, swishing the water until it's lukewarm, then rummage through the kitchen cabinets until I find a packet of oatmeal. I hope the instant microwaveable kind counts.

I lower myself into the tub and stretch out so that every part of me except my face is underwater. The oatmeal flakes float to the surface.

My cell phone is on the bathmat by the tub so I can see it. But Mick doesn't call or text. Where can he be?

I close my eyes and try to relax. But when I do, I picture that guy at Scoops and hear the sound of his fingers snapping. When I open my eyes, I see the hives on my belly. They don't seem to be getting any smaller, but at least I'm not so itchy now. I scratch my belly, but this time I'm careful to use just my fingertips, not my nails.

I make myself stay in the tub for fifteen minutes. Mick still hasn't phoned. I hope he won't go all the way downtown to pick me up and then not find me there. When he does phone, I'll ask him if he minds stopping at the pharmacy and getting me some antihistamines.

I dry myself carefully, dabbing at my skin instead of toweling myself dry the way I usually do. *Poor you*, I think. *You've had a rough night.*

I put on Mick's softest T-shirt—it's 100 percent cotton. He likes it when I wear pretty camis, but right now I couldn't bear anything lacy on my skin. I'm still itchy, but I'm trying not to scratch. I think the oatmeal has helped, even if it was the instant kind.

I'm sitting on the couch, rereading *Hamlet* (or trying to), when I hear Mick opening the door to the loft. "Joey!" he says too loudly. "You here?"

"Uh-huh," I answer in a small voice. I don't have the energy to get up from the couch. "I tried your cell.

Did you go pick me up? I tried to tell you not to bother. I'm sorry if you did."

Mick is standing in front of me now. I smell wine on his breath. Why has he been out drinking when he told me he'd be here reviewing scripts? And who was he with? I can't read the look in his dark eyes. He's either concerned—or angry. Please don't be angry now, I think, willing him to read my mind. I can't take any more anger—especially not tonight.

"Damn cell phone's out of juice," he says, pulling the phone out of his jeans pocket and showing it to me as if I don't know what he means. "I was there at eleven fifteen sharp at the corner. When you weren't out at eleven thirty, I went in to see what was going on. That other waitress—what's her name again? Joyce?—she told me you got into some trouble. So I came right home, figuring you'd come here."

When Mick opens his arms, spreading them wide, I know he's not angry. No, he wants to comfort me. So I stand up and let myself fall into his arms. "I quit," I tell him. "Some guy was super rude to me and I lost it."

Mick presses me close and strokes my back. Ah, this feels so good, so right—like heaven, if there's a heaven. He cradles me and whispers into my ear, "You did the right thing, Joey. It was a lousy job anyway. It was beneath you."

I can practically feel the hives starting to go back to wherever they came from. I don't say anything about Mick's wine breath—or ask him where he's been and who he was with. And I don't mention the restraining order or the poem either. Now's not the time.

~

In the morning, I'm awake before Mick. There's no sign of the hives—not even any scratch marks on my skin. Outside, the sky is still rosy and everything feels possible. Mick's right—that job was beneath me. I was right to quit.

I put the kettle on for tea and give William Shakespeare his breakfast. I'm careful not to make too much noise, because I don't want to wake Mick. In a little while, I'll go next door to feed Sunshine.

I bring my cup of tea over to the couch. Mick's cell phone is on the coffee table. He's forgotten to recharge it. When I pick it up to plug it in, the screen lights up. I check the battery level. The phone's not out of juice at all.

CHAPTER 23

"Then is doomsday near."
—*HAMLET*, ACT 2, SCENE 2

When I go next door, I'm startled to find Mrs. Karpman sitting in her velvet chair. Because she isn't wearing pantyhose, I can see the deep-purple veins in her legs. She's rubbing her forehead. Maybe she has a sinus infection. She's mentioned that she gets them sometimes. That would also explain why she's home a day early from Toronto.

"Is something wrong?" I call out as I slip off my shoes (Mrs. Karpman is particular about her floors). "I thought you weren't getting home till tomorrow." When she realizes I'm there, she looks confused, almost as if she doesn't know who I am. "It's me, Iris," I say. "I came to feed Sunshine."

"Oh, Iris," she says. "Of course." I don't usually notice the lines on Mrs. Karpman's face, but this morning I do. Maybe it's because of the way the sun is shining in through her windows. Or maybe it's because she hasn't put on the shimmery face powder she usually wears.

"Oh, Iris," she says again, shaking her head this time. "I cut my trip short because I had the oddest feeling that I needed to come home—and I was right. Something terrible has happened."

I bring my hand to my mouth. "It's not Sunshine, is it?" I know how much she loves her bird.

Sunshine chirps when I say his name. Phew. I'd have felt awful if he had gotten sick—or died—while I was looking after him.

"What's wrong?" I hope no one in Mrs. Karpman's family is sick.

At first, Mrs. Karpman doesn't say anything. I wish she'd stop shaking her head like that. It's making me nervous. When she finally speaks, her voice sounds exhausted—as if she hasn't slept in days. "The apartment's been robbed. All my jewelry's gone." Now I notice the rims of her eyes are red, like Sunshine's. She's probably been crying. "Every piece was a gift from my Nelson," she says softly.

My heart is breaking open. I go over and give her the biggest hug I can. Her shoulders are bony, and she feels like a small bird in my arms. "How could it have happened?" I ask. "I was here yesterday morning and everything was fine. I double-checked the door when I left, the way I always do." Though I haven't done anything wrong,

I still feel guilty. I was responsible for Mrs. Karpman's apartment while she was away.

"The apartment looked fine to me, too, when I came home last night," she says, and I can tell she's making an effort to collect herself. "At least, at first. I only noticed something was wrong when I was getting ready for bed. Whoever robbed me went straight to my bedroom—and to the jewelry box on my dresser. I think he knew what he was looking for. That's what the police think too. I suppose it could have been worse. Imagine if I'd walked in on him!" Mrs. Karpman shuts her eyes. "I'd have had a heart attack!"

"But how did a burglar get in here? The lock wasn't broken, was it?"

"Probably with a credit card. According to the police, that's what burglars use nowadays. I phoned the police as soon as I noticed someone had emptied my jewelry box. I tried knocking on your door, but you two were out. The police say this sort of thing happens a lot in apartment buildings. Especially ones with old people in them." Mrs. Karpman sighs. "They told me I need to compile a list. For the insurance company. But I can't think straight, Iris. I just can't get over the idea that someone was in here— prowling and going through my personal things." Mrs. Karpman shudders.

"I'm so sorry."

"Don't be silly, Iris. You have nothing to be sorry for."
Does Mrs. Karpman give me a funny look when she says
that? I hope she doesn't think I'm responsible! But when
I look at her again, the funny look is gone. I must have
imagined it. "By the way, dear, I nearly forgot to thank
you—for looking after Sunshine."

Sunshine chirps again when Mrs. Karpman says his
name. That makes us both laugh a little. I'm glad to see
Mrs. Karpman's face relax. "I can stay and help you with
the list. If you think that would help."

"That would be wonderful. You're a darling girl. Let
me put on some tea."

I watch Mrs. Karpman as she shuffles into her kitchen
and plugs in the kettle. "How would you like to use this
teacup?" she asks, showing me a blue-and-white cup with
a windmill on it. "We bought it when we were in Delft. In
Holland." As we wait for the water to boil, Mrs. Karpman
looks into Sunshine's cage. "It's a shame you don't speak
English," I hear her tell the bird. "If you did, you could tell
us who took my jewelry."

Mrs. Karpman keeps remembering more pieces of
jewelry. Her pearl necklace (she tears up a little when she
mentions it; Nelson bought it for her when they were on
a river cruise in China), several gold brooches, a diamond
tennis bracelet ("I should have worn it to Toronto and then
I'd still have it," she says), a pearl ring ("I wanted to give

it to Sarah, my eldest granddaughter, when she turned sixteen"), her good watch. "Write down that it was eighteen-karat gold, a Longines," she says, watching over my shoulder to see that I'm following her instructions.

Mrs. Karpman bites her lip when she remembers that Nelson's pocket watch is missing too. "He adored that watch. I bought it at Birks. He said it always reminded him that time was precious." I don't tell her I've already heard the story of the watch and how she bought it for Nelson's fiftieth birthday. "I'd been planning to give the watch to Errol." Mrs. Karpman's voice breaks. "Have I told you he's coming to Montreal?"

I shake out my arm. The list is getting quite long. "No, you didn't mention it."

"When I phoned my children to tell them about the break-in, they got very upset. Between you and me, Iris, I think they're just looking for an excuse to move me to an old folks' home. They're sending Errol to check on me." Mrs. Karpman makes a *harrmphing* sound. "To think how many times I babysat that boy. And now they seem to think *I* need a babysitter! Enjoy your youth, Iris, that's all I can say."

"When's he coming?"

"When's who coming?"

Now I start to worry that Mrs. Karpman is losing her marbles. "Errol. You told me he's coming to look in on you."

"Oh yes, Errol. He'll be here in time for dinner. Which reminds me, I need to phone the butcher shop and get them to deliver an extra large grain-fed capon. My Errol eats enough for two people."

At least the thought of Errol eating her extra large grain-fed capon makes Mrs. Karpman smile.

Mick is standing by the window, stretching, when I get back from Mrs. Karpman's. He turns to look at me. "Where were you?" he asks sleepily.

"Over at Mrs. Karpman's. Her apartment got broken into. She thinks it happened yesterday."

Mick crosses his arms over his chest. "That's awful. What did they take?"

"Mostly jewelry, I think. I feel terrible about it." William Shakespeare is brushing his head against my leg, and I lean down to pet him.

Mick walks to the kitchen and puts two slices of whole-wheat bread into the toaster. "Why in the world should you feel terrible about it, Joey?" he asks as he reaches into the pantry for the jam he likes.

"Well, I was supposed to be looking after the apartment. I hope she doesn't think I did it."

Mick yawns. "That's the most ridiculous thing I ever heard. Sometimes I honestly wonder what's wrong with you, Joey. Why you feel so damned responsible for everything.

Come on over here and have some toast, will you?" It's a question, but it doesn't feel like one.

I take a tiny bite of toast. Even if I don't have much of an appetite.

"So tell me exactly what happened at work yesterday," Mick says.

If I talk about it, I'll have to relive the whole scene. Then again, I might as well get this over with. "Some guy snapped his fingers at me and, well—" I stop to find the right words. "I went kinda crazy…I dumped one of those tubs of dirty dishes over him."

I watch Mick's face as I tell the story. I want him to laugh, because I'm realizing that though it didn't seem funny when it happened, it makes a good story now. What I really want is for Mick to tell me I did the right thing, but so far he's not reacting. His face is perfectly blank. So I keep talking. "I think I'd had it with that job—with being disrespected." It's only when I say it that I realize that's exactly why I lost it. "What did you say last night… that the job was beneath me?"

Mick raises his eyebrows. "I said that?" I can't tell if he's being serious or teasing me. "I must've had too much to drink. You made good money at that job, Joey."

My eyes are glued to Mick's face. For the first time since I met him, I have the weird feeling that I don't really know him. I love him, I'm sure of that, but I don't *really really* know him. What goes on inside his head? Why does he sometimes get so angry? Are there more secrets he is keeping from me?

I think about Mrs. Karpman's key in Mick's kitchen drawer. I think about what Mick made me do at Forever 21. What I did at Forever 21. I haven't been able to wear any of those clothes, not even the maxi dress I liked so much. Just seeing those clothes in the closet makes my stomach lurch.

"You didn't do it, did you?" I blurt out.

Mick wipes his mouth with the inside of his hand. "What are you talking about, Joey?"

"You didn't rob Mrs. Karpman, did you?"

"How could you ask me that?" Mick's eyes are turning wild again, and I wish I could take back the question. But it's too late. I'm watching his hands, and instinctively I pull back a little from the table.

One of Mick's hands is moving in slow motion. Or maybe it's not that his hand is moving slowly but that my brain is slowing the moment down, splitting it into separate frames.

I watch as the back of Mick's hand sweeps the dishes off the table. Our two plates, our teacups, the sugar bowl and the jam jar too.

"Stop it!" I raise my voice so he'll hear me over the sound of the clattering dishes. When I look down at the floor,

I see that the plates have not broken, but the sugar bowl has shattered into a thousand pieces and there is sugar everywhere. I get up to find the dustpan and a wet cloth. If I don't clean this mess up right away, the whole floor will get sticky. I don't ever want to walk on another sticky floor.

"Why should I stop it?" Mick yells. "What do you think I am? Who do you think I am? Do you honestly think I'd rob an old woman?"

I know I shouldn't fight. I know I should let Mick do whatever he has to do to spend his anger. But it's getting harder for me to just stand by and do nothing. "I know you'd rob a clothing store. Or make me rob one," I say.

"That's different," Mick says. "Completely different."

"No, it's not. It's not different at all!" I'm yelling now too. I know I shouldn't. That yelling will only make things worse. But I can't help it. The dustpan flies out of my hands.

He punches me again. Same spot. On the right side of my face. Why does he always aim for the same spot? It's weird the things you think about when something terrible is happening. He punches me so hard I can feel my teeth breaking through the soft skin inside my mouth. So hard I taste blood. The taste is flat, like metal, but somehow not unpleasant.

Why is everything happening in slow motion again? It's as if I'm watching my life on the screen, or in a play. As if it's all happening to someone else. A girl who happens to be named Iris Wagner, a girl I hardly know anymore.

I've dropped to my knees. I'm too winded to stand. Mick is glaring at me. Why is he looking at me as if I'm the one who's done something wrong? "Maybe you shouldn't have quit that job," he mutters.

It hurts to talk. But there's something else I want to say. And I don't care if it makes him angrier. "I found the restraining order—and that poem," I tell him, looking straight into his eyes. "The one you said you wrote for me."

Mick shakes his head. I'm sure he's going to punch me again, but I don't care. I feel like I have nothing more to lose. Let him punch me.

CHAPTER 24

"How weary, stale, flat, and unprofitable
Seem to me all the uses of this world!"
—HAMLET, ACT 1, SCENE 2

Afterward.

I am sitting hunched on the closet floor, rocking back and forth, hugging myself.

Every inch of me aches. My arms, my legs and especially the skin around my nose and cheek. I lift one finger to my cheekbone, but at the last second I pull my hand away. The skin is too tender to touch, and it's so hot I can feel the heat even without touching it.

There's a ringing in my skull that feels like it will never stop. Boom, boom, boom. Like an angry church bell.

Even though it's over now and my heart isn't thumping triple-time the way it was before, I can't stop picturing his fingers. Long thin fingers balled into a tight fist, coming at me like a cannon. And the rage in his eyes. Why, I wonder for the first time, don't I ever fight back? What is it about me that makes me feel so helpless, so paralyzed, when Mick loses it?

Cartoonists draw stars around someone who gets punched. The funny thing is, when you get punched in real life, you actually see stars. Silver and gold stars ricocheting off each other like fireworks. That's what it's like for me anyway. I wonder how the cartoonists figured it out. Did they all get punched in the head too?

I want to cry. I want to let everything out—my sorrow, my disappointment in myself, in Mick, in us, how lost and overwhelmed and small I feel—but I have no tears left. Not one. There's a desert in my head.

I hear Mick moving around the apartment, making normal sounds. I strain my ears to hear better. He's taking something out of a drawer, clearing his throat, closing the drawer, opening up his laptop, humming. How can he be humming? He knows where I am. Besides the bathroom, this closet is the only place to hide.

But I don't expect him to come and talk to me now or say he's sorry. He's regrouping. The way I am doing in the closet. It's what we do after a terrible fight—and there's no question, this one was a terrible fight, not a squabble.

When I'm ready, I'll come out. I'll go to the bathroom and assess the damage the way a mechanic would after a car wreck. I'll make another cold compress and hold it over the achy spots. If the skin is broken, I'll put on Polysporin. In a strange way, I am getting good at this.

Then Mick and I will be able to start over fresh. I'll say I'm sorry I got so upset, that I should never have accused him of robbing Mrs. Karpman, that the restraining order and the poem—the one he said he wrote for me but that he wrote for Millicent—don't mean anything. They're no big deal. Millicent is crazy. I know she is. And the poem— well, it was just a silly poem. I'll explain to Mick how I'm PMSing big time and how I'll try to be better. And not upset him so much. Especially now, when he is under so much pressure from the lawyer and the new play in Quebec City. No wonder he keeps losing it. Artists are sensitive people. They feel things for the rest of us. That's why they're so important to society. I need to find a way to support Mick better. If I'm better, he'll be better. I know it.

How could I have ever even thought he'd rob Mrs. Karpman? The business at Forever 21 was different. Forever 21 is a huge corporation. We were being like Robin Hood in Sherwood Forest. Robbing the rich. Even if we weren't exactly helping the poor. No, Mick would never rob Mrs. Karpman. He knows what good friends she and I have become.

Thinking about *later* helps. Thinking about *now*... well...it hurts too much to think about. I've never felt so lonely. Even lonelier than when I've been completely, totally alone with no one to talk to and nothing to do. More lonely than when I was little and I'd let myself into the empty house before Mom got back from organizing other people's lives.

There's a meow outside the closet door. William Shakespeare is pushing his soft marmalade body against the folding door. I lean forward and open the door just a little so he can come inside. The cat nudges his head against my shin and meows again. He wants me to pet him. At first, I don't. I can't. But when he meows again, I do. The feel of his soft, warm fur makes me feel a little better. Creature comfort.

William Shakespeare has been a witness to almost every one of our arguments. He must have noticed I'm trembling, because now he's trembling too. In sympathy, I'll bet. Which makes me feel sorry for upsetting him. "It's okay, don't worry," I whisper. "Everything'll be okay. I promise." I need to make things better. Not just for me, but for William Shakespeare too. The little cat depends on me.

It's the feel of William Shakespeare's fur brushing against me and the sound of his steady purring when I stroke the spot between his eyes that make me cry. But I cover my mouth with one hand to muffle the sound. Still hunched, I keep rocking my body back and forth. I'm so lost and so little. I don't know how I will ever find my way again.

Shhh, I tell myself. *If Mick hears you cry, he'll only get angry all over again.*

William Shakespeare and I are still in the closet when I hear Mick getting ready to leave. He pauses for a few seconds outside the closet door—he knows we're in here— and I think maybe he's going to say something. That he's going to break the terrible, tense silence hanging in the air like a sour smell.

Maybe this time things will be different, and he'll apologize. My heart lifts a little at the thought. "Joey," he'll say, and I imagine him getting down on his knees, his eyes welling up with tears, "I can't believe what I just did—how I hurt you. I'm so sorry. So deeply, deeply sorry. Can you forgive me, Joey? I swear it will never ever happen again. I've been such a fool!" I'll wipe his tears away. Comfort him. Tell him that yes, of course I forgive him. That I could forgive him anything. That's what love is, isn't it?

I know he can hear me breathing and William Shakespeare purring (stroking the cat is making me feel a little better), but Mick doesn't say anything. Not a word. Nothing. The air smells even more sour.

When Mick leaves, he slams the door behind him. So hard the folding closet door rattles.

I could leave the closet now, but I'm still not ready. It feels safer to keep hugging myself and crying in here. Even though Mick has left—where has he gone, and who

was he with last night?—I'm careful not to sob too loudly.
What if Mrs. Karpman goes to drop her garbage down the
chute and hears me from the hallway?

I don't know how much later it is when I finally get up
and go to the bathroom. It could be minutes, it could be
an hour. Time has contracted or expanded. I don't know
which. I don't care which.

I should have started icing my face right away. I look
worse than god-awful. No makeup job will hide the damage
this time. The skin around my right eye is so swollen, I can't
even open it all the way. I trudge to the freezer for ice, then
wrap the cubes inside a washcloth and make an extra-
strength, extra-cold compress. I press it to my cheek until I
can't bear the sting any longer.

I try lying down. Somehow, I don't know how, I manage
to fall asleep. I dream I'm back in that dark forest with the
too-tall trees and no way out. The feeling of hopelessness
is still with me when I hear knocking. At first, I think it's
part of my dream. A woodpecker pecking away high up
in one of those too-tall trees. The bird is trying to tell me
something.

But no, it's someone knocking on the door to the loft.
I get up, still groggy, clutching my face. It must be Mick.
But why is he knocking? Maybe he's brought me a bouquet
of pale purple irises and his hands are so full, he can't get

to his key. He wants to make up with me, I know he does.

"Mick, is that you?" I ask from my side of the door.

"No, it isn't," an unfamiliar voice says. There's a moment of silence. "My name's Errol. I think you know my bubbie, Mrs. Karpman. She lives next door."

Oh no. Errol. And because I've already said something, it's too late to pretend there's no one home. I need to make Errol go away.

"Uh," I say, scrambling to come up with some excuse, "I'm kind of busy right now."

"Look," he says—I can't help noticing that Errol has a kind voice, a steady reliable voice, and because I have seen his photo in his grandmother's living room, I can picture his face too—"I'm sorry to bug you, Iris. But my bubbie says she doesn't have your phone number. She says she thinks your, uh, boyfriend went out this afternoon... and that you're all alone in there...and, well, she wants to know if you want to come for supper. She's making roast chicken. With potatoes. Look, are you going to open the door or what? It feels a little weird standing out here having a conversation with a door, if you know what I mean."

I smile when he says that. But only for a second. Smiling hurts.

"Errol, look, I'm really sorry, but I can't open the door right now. It's too complicated to explain. And I can't come for dinner either. But tell your bubbie thanks from me, will you? Tell her I'll see her in a few days. And maybe I'll get to meet you next time, okay?"

I can almost hear Errol thinking outside the door. He's quiet for a few seconds and then he says, "Okay, if you say so. I just hope you're all right in there."

"I'm fine," I lie.

"Okay then. Maybe next time. And if you change your mind about the chicken, just come by. Bubbie would like it."

I hear Mrs. Karpman's apartment door click open and shut. Thank goodness I got rid of Errol. Still, I think, as I go back to the freezer for some fresh ice, it would've been nice to meet him. If he's anything like his bubbie, I'm sure I'd like him.

There's more knocking a few hours later. This time, I don't say anything. I know it isn't Mick—and I just want Errol to go away. I can't handle another awkward conversation. What I need to do is figure out how to drop out of my usual life for a few days—I can't go anywhere looking like this. This time, no one would believe me even if I said I'd bumped into a Mack truck.

But it's not Errol. It's Mrs. Karpman. And I smell roast chicken. I must be feeling a little better, because I'm suddenly hungry. "Iris," Mrs. Karpman says, and her voice sounds even more strained than usual. "I know you're in there, dear. And I know you're in trouble. I understand if you don't want to come for supper. Maybe you're just not up to it. Iris, can you hear me?"

"Uh-huh," I say. I didn't mean to say anything; the *uh-huh* just slipped out.

"Okay, that's good. Iris, I want you to know that I'm leaving you a plate out here with chicken and potatoes. I want you to eat it and I want you to feel better. You're a sweet girl, Iris, and you deserve only good things. You're going to eat the chicken, aren't you, dear?"

"Uh-huh," I say again. I'm getting kind of choked up. It's not just the thought of Mrs. Karpman bringing me dinner; it's also what she said about my deserving only good things. Part of me thinks she's right. Part of me isn't so sure. "Thanks," I manage to say.

"You're very welcome, dear. And keep the plate until you come to visit me again."

I expect to hear Mrs. Karpman going back into her apartment, but I don't. She is still standing outside Mick's door.

"I need to go now," I tell her.

"Iris," she says, "I want to call the police."

Everything inside me clenches up. "Don't do that. Please, Mrs. Karpman. Don't."

"You're putting me in a terrible position," Mrs. Karpman says. "And I want the best for you, Iris, really I do." It sounds like Mrs. Karpman is about to cry.

"I'm sorry," I tell her. "I really am. But please, I'm begging you, don't phone the police."

"All right then," Mrs. Karpman says. Her voice sounds tired, and I'm sorry I've made her worry, put her in a bad position. "But you let that man know I'm keeping an eye on both of you."

CHAPTER 25

"By indirections find directions out."
—*HAMLET*, ACT 2, SCENE 1

I've told so many lies in the last week, I'm having trouble keeping track of them all. I'm like a juggler with too many balls in the air, grinning like crazy at the audience during my performance but worried sick inside that one of my juggling balls—or all of them—is going to come crashing down on my head and roll right off the stage. And then what will everyone think?

I told my mom that Katie's parents were out of town all week and that she was afraid to stay in the house by herself, so I needed to stay over there. Mom wasn't too happy, but I promised I'd make it up to her once we were done with the play. I also told her rehearsals had been going really late so I'd get more sleep if I stayed at Katie's. "I'm feeling kind of worn out," I told her, which was the only part of my story that was true.

"I know how much you need your sleep," Mom said, "so I'm going to say okay. But once this play is over, Iris, I want you to start spending more time at home. I won't have you running yourself ragged. A person needs a balanced lifestyle." I didn't point out that *balanced* wasn't the first word I'd use to describe *her* lifestyle.

I emailed Ms. Cameron to say I had an awful flu and was probably highly contagious and that I was really, really sorry but I'd have to miss the dress rehearsal, and could someone stand in for me—maybe Katie, or maybe even Ms. Cameron herself? I also promised Ms. Cameron that I was working on my lines (that part was true too) and that I'd be totally ready for the performance.

I didn't expect Ms. Cameron to email me back, but she did. She wanted to know if I needed anything, anything at all. She even suggested dropping by for a visit, which I thought was a strange offer, considering she's my teacher. I nixed that plan. *I'd never forgive myself*, I wrote to her, *if you caught this flu. What if you couldn't be there for* Hamlet?

I even posted my having the flu on Facebook, in case anyone from school checked. (Thank God Mom isn't one of those parents with a Facebook account.) And I told Mick I forgave him (not that he apologized or that I still expect him to). Anyway, that was also a lie because inside, I haven't forgiven him. Not this time. I want to and I plan to—how else can we move forward as a couple?—but I'm just not there yet. Soon, I hope.

At least my face is pretty much back to normal. I think all the icing helped, and maybe also the fact that I've been getting a ton of rest. I didn't know a person could sleep so much. I've been tired in a way I'm not used to—as if it's not just my muscles and bones that are tired but also my brain and even my heart, if that's possible. I wake up tired in the morning and after every nap. The thought of tonight's performance exhausts me all over again. How am I going to get through it?

I start feeling more alive once I leave the loft. Maybe it wasn't the best idea to stay cooped up in there all week like some sick chicken. The April air feels soft against my skin. The daffodils are in full golden bloom. That means the irises will be next.

When I straighten my shoulders, I realize I've been hunched up like an old person. *Shoulders back,* I tell myself. *Take a long deep breath. Breathe out the old stale air and fill your lungs with fresh spring air. Aaah, doesn't that feel good?* It's as if I can hear Ms. Cameron's voice inside my head.

Katie's waiting by the school entrance. She lifts her wrist to show me she's wearing her bracelet. I wish I'd remembered to wear mine.

"Did you lose weight?" she asks when I get to where she's standing. "I sure wish I'd catch the flu. Come over here and breathe on me, will you? Maybe you've still got some skinny germs left."

Ms. Cameron is directing traffic in the hallway. "Let's go, people!" she calls out. "You need to be in your costumes in ten minutes. Hey, Iris, how are you feeling?" she asks when I try to slither past her. "Did you beat that flu?" I can't tell whether Ms. Cameron is giving me a suspicious look or if it's just that her eyebrows are plucked so thin. And did she pause for a second after she said the word *beat*?

Ms. Cameron beckons to me, and I stop beside her. "My friend Marilyn mentioned she saw you and Mick Horton together. She thinks he's been helping you with your lines. Outside of school, I gather. Is that true, Iris?"

"Uh..." I don't know how much I'm allowed to tell her. I decide to go for part of the truth this time. Leaving things out is easier for me than lying. "He's helped me," I say, doing my best to look her in the eye without flinching. "Once or twice."

Ms. Cameron shifts from one foot to the other. It looks like it's her turn to decide how much to say. She runs her hand over my shoulder. "You be careful with him," she tells me. "He's a talented man, but he can be"—she stops to choose the next word—"temperamental. Now go get your costume on."

All the actors are wearing black bodysuits. That was Mick's idea. He says it reinforces the play's themes of isolation and madness.

I'm wearing a flowing black dress over my bodysuit. The dress is made of rayon, but it feels like silk. It used to be Ms. Cameron's, and when I wear it, I feel grown up and sexy. It fits tight at the chest but falls loose from the waist.

Tommy is backstage, busy on his laptop. He looks up when he sees me. "Hey, Iris, glad you're over that flu. Break a leg tonight, okay?"

"What are you working on?" Making conversation helps me forget how jittery I am, though Mick says jitters are good—they make a performance edgier and more authentic.

"I'm putting the finishing touches on the director's note. Wanna see?"

The lettering on the note is in white on a black background. "It looks really dramatic," I tell Tommy, and he looks pleased.

"Thanks. Too bad it's such total bullshit."

"What do you mean?"

Tommy reads from the computer screen in a nasal old man's voice. (He should have auditioned for Polonius's role.) "'Tonight's production leaves space for the audience to make its own psychological and spiritual discoveries. My job as director has been to guide the arc of my performers' experience.'" Tommy shrugs. "I mean, can you imagine Ms. Cameron spewing that kind of BS? It's totally that dude Horton."

"You're right," is all I say. "It doesn't sound like Ms. Cameron."

Ms. Cameron is backstage now, giving us our final instructions. "Think of yourselves as professionals," she says, her hands planted on her hips. "You've worked for this and you're ready for it. And by the way, there are a lot of people out there."

When the curtains *swish* open, I am watching from the wings. I see my mom sitting in the front row. There's an empty seat next to her. I suck in my breath when someone comes in late and takes the spot. Oh my god, it's Mick. How weird is that? I watch as my mom gives him a friendly nod and rearranges her knees to give him more room. Next thing I know, she'll be handing him her business card and asking if he needs his closets organized.

I spot Katie's and Tommy's parents too, three rows behind my mom and Mick.

There's some spooky harpsichord music that Tommy found online, and then the play begins.

Shakespeare is a total genius. I'm not just saying that because it's what Mick thinks. It's my own opinion too. I love the way Shakespeare starts the play with the ghost. Talk about a hook! And the language—it's simple and complex at the same time. Mick calls it *multi-layered*. Shakespeare's words have a way of staying in your mind, and your mind keeps going over them, understanding them better, seeing more in them. His plays make you bigger than you were before you saw or read them.

I swear I get shivers when Francisco says, "'Tis bitter cold, and I am sick at heart.'" I have this feeling I will never forget those words ever—that they're becoming part of me. I think back to last week's blowout with Mick and how I felt when I was hiding in the closet afterward. That's it exactly. I was *sick at heart*. Did Shakespeare know that feeling too? He must've, or else he'd never have been able to write that line. I think maybe I still am sick at heart. Mick's been gentle with me all week, and he's been helping around the loft—straightening things up, warming up soup for dinner—and never once raising his voice, but that sick-at-heart feeling won't go away.

In most productions of *Hamlet*, Ophelia wears white because she's associated with innocence and virginity. Someone in the audience—is it my mom?—gasps when I walk onto the stage.

As I make my way to center stage, I can hear my father's voice inside my head. *Go for it, Iris*, he's telling me. *Really go for it!* I shut my eyes as I prepare to say my lines. Mentally, I thank my father for his support. Even if he hasn't been much of a father to me, the fact that he believes in me now—well, it helps.

When I say my lines, the most wonderful, incredible thing happens: I'm her. Ophelia. One hundred percent Ophelia. There's no room left tonight for Iris. And I'm glad of it. I've had too much Iris lately.

It's a long production—nearly two hours, with no intermission. A few small things go wrong (the harp music starts playing when it shouldn't; Lenore forgets two of her lines, not that I mind that glitch). Still, the play hangs together.

The cast comes out to take a group bow, and the audience gives us a standing ovation. It's weird to see my mom and Mick standing so close together. I notice that my mom's got a bouquet of irises in her arms.

"Iris, I'm afraid I haven't given you enough credit," she tells me afterward. "You were fabulous tonight. You were all fabulous."

Mick is hovering behind her, watching the two of us. He has an amused expression on his face. "Uh, Mom," I say, "I'd like you to meet Mick Horton. He's, uh, a friend of Ms. Cameron's. Mr. Horton, this is my mom." I can't believe I've just called my boyfriend Mr. Horton.

Mick doesn't seem to think any of this is weird. "Good to meet you, Mrs. Wagner," he says, taking her hand and holding on to it a little too long. I really hope he isn't flirting with my mom. "Iris really takes after you," Mick says. "You're both lovely."

I don't think I've ever seen Mom blush before.

"Do I detect an Australian accent?" she asks him.

As if things aren't awkward enough, I see Katie's parents walking toward us. Her mom is waving. "You were a marvelous Ophelia," I hear her saying. "So full of emotion." I'm not nuts about leaving my mom and Mick alone together (what if she says something really goofy?), but I also know I need to intercept Katie's parents.

"Will you excuse me for a second?" I say to Mom and Mick. "Hey, Mrs. Carsley." I try blocking Katie's mom's way, but it's like trying to block a giant green recycling truck when it comes barreling down your street.

Mrs. Carsley kisses the air on both sides of my face. "The person I really want to congratulate is your mom. I know she's raised you alone, so I think it's especially important to tell someone like that"—she makes it sound as if single motherhood is a fatal disease—"what a wonderful job she's done."

"Alice!" Mrs. Carsley bustles over to my mom. "It's been ages. Your Iris was simply marvelous. You've done a wonderful job. And to think you've done it all alone." Mrs. Carsley pats the padded shoulder of her husband's suit as if the man inside is a well-behaved pet.

To my mom's credit, she doesn't get annoyed. Instead, she smiles graciously—and for the first time I wonder if maybe she should have gone into acting too. "Thanks, Elizabeth.

It's very kind of you to say so. By the way, I heard the two of you were out of town this week. Iris didn't mention where you went."

Mrs. Carsley purses her lips. She shoots me a look, and for a second I have the weird feeling she's going to cover for me.

But in the end, Mrs. Carsley isn't the problem. It's Mr. Carsley. "Away? Not us," he says, shrugging his padded shoulders. "We haven't been out of town since Christmas. Though it's high time we planned something, don't you think, Elizabeth?"

Mom's eyes get really wide. "If you'll excuse us," she says to the Carsleys and to Mick, who is still hanging around. Then she tugs my hand—hard—and practically drags me over to the side of the room. "Iris," she hisses, "what in God's name is going on? Talk to me, Iris! Now!" Her green eyes are flashing in a way I'm not used to. She looks worried and angry. Mostly angry. I'm afraid she's going to shake me.

When I step back, she takes two steps toward me. We're so close now, I feel her breath on my face.

"I'm really sorry, Mom," I say, "but I can't talk now." I can't back up any farther, so I point at all the people milling about. Some of them are already watching us. "Not with everyone here. And the cast party starts in fifteen minutes. I can't miss it, Mom."

"The cast party? Have you lost your mind? Whatever is going on here between us is way more important than some cast party! There's no excuse, Iris Wagner, for deceiving me. I don't know what's been going on with you lately, young lady, but we're going to get to the bottom of it. *Now!*"

She's grabbing at my hand again. I shake it loose. I can't stand anyone touching me in an aggressive way.

"I'll tell you everything tomorrow—I swear I will," I say, meeting Mom's eyes.

"No, you won't." She hasn't taken my hand again, but it's as if she's holding on to me with her eyes. "You'll tell me everything right now. I don't care who can see us."

I can't keep talking to her now. Not like this. I need time to get my story straight. To figure out which lies I can undo. "Look, I'm really, really sorry, Mom, I swear I am. I shouldn't have lied to you. But you need to understand— things are pretty weird for me right now." I work to keep my voice calm, thinking maybe that'll help to calm her down too.

"*Pretty weird right now?* What on earth are you talking about, Iris Wagner?" I wish she wouldn't keep calling me *Iris Wagner* like that.

"Do I look like an idiot to you?" she's asking now. She is getting herself even more worked up. Soon the whole school will know we're fighting.

"No. No, you don't. Not at all," I whisper, hoping she will take my cue and lower her voice.

"Do I look like a pushover? Do I? Tell me that, Iris Wagner."

"No, definitely not."

I can see Mick hovering in the distance. His eyebrows are raised. He must know my mom has figured something out.

"Tomorrow," I tell her again. "I'll explain tomorrow. Please, Mom, just give me till then."

"Iris"—and now the look in my mom's eyes gets even fiercer—"you and I are having a problem, a *big* problem, today. Right here. Right now. So you'd better come clean with me." She has finally lowered her voice, and I know it's because she is about to pull out the heavy ammunition. "After everything we've been through, Iris, you owe me the truth."

The word *truth* hits me like a kick in the stomach. It hits me so hard I nearly give in. I nearly tell her everything. *The truth.* Only now, something else occurs to me: Mom hasn't always told *me* the truth. She's angry with me, but I realize I'm angry with her too—and I have a right to be. But why does it feel so scary to be angry with her? Maybe it's because it's a feeling I've never allowed myself. Maybe I've never dared to be angry with her. Because I've needed her so much.

Mick is coming closer. I can feel it even without looking up at him.

I meet my mom's eyes. "You know what, Mom? You owe me the truth too." I'm shaking.

"What are you talking about, Iris?" There's something else now in my mom's eyes. Not anger. Recognition. Maybe even a hint of fear.

"Tomorrow." I say it in my firmest voice. I'm still a little shaky.

Mom sighs, and I notice how tired she looks. Usually, I'd feel guilty.

Then she gives a half-nod. I can tell she's trying to get a grip, to come up with a plan the way she might come up with a plan to organize a closet full of junk. "All right, Iris," she says, "but you're going to have to tell me one thing right now—before you go to any party. Just one thing." Mom sucks in her breath. "Are you in some kind of serious trouble, Iris? Are you?"

This time it's harder work to meet her eyes. "It's nothing I can't deal with," I tell her. I'm afraid my voice will break, but somehow it doesn't.

～

I freak out a little when, just before it's time to leave for the cast party, Mick sidles over and tells me we're going to need to lie low for a while. "It's obvious," he whispers, "that your mother is getting suspicious."

"What does *lie low* mean?" I don't care that I sound desperate.

"It means we don't see each other for a few days."

"I can't. I won't." I didn't tear up before, but now I do.

"You have to. It won't be for long, Joey. I can't have other people finding out about us. Not yet. You've got to understand. I—I've got too much to lose."

"I don't want to be without you," I sputter. "Ever."

Mick touches the tip of my nose. "Me neither, Joey…"

"I thought you loved me so much it hurts." If that reminds Mick of the poem, he doesn't say anything about it.

"I do. We'll talk in the morning. You go ahead without me to the party. I'm going back to the loft to look at the script those guys from Quebec City sent me. And Joey, when you talk to your mother tomorrow"—Mick looks at me as if to underline the importance of what he's about to say—"don't mention anything about us. Not a word. Got that?"

I feel as lost as I do in my dreams, when I'm in that dark forest. "What do I tell her then?" I need Mick's help. I'm out of stories.

"Tell her you've been with that kid. The one you were going out with before we got together."

I nod my head, but now I've got even more lies to try and keep straight. Now I could fill two notebooks with lies.

The cast party is at Lenore's. She lives in a huge white brick house in Hampstead. It has a circular driveway, and inside it's full of antiques. Someone's left the front door open, so I let myself in. Because the first floor has an open plan, I see right away that everyone's there: Katie, Tommy, Antoine and all the others from the cast and crew. Everyone but Mick. I can't stop thinking how much more fun it would be if he was here. Even if we had to pretend we weren't together.

Tommy is hanging his jacket up on the antique coatrack. "Hey, Ophelia," he says when he sees me. "You were really something tonight."

Someone hands me a beer.

Lenore doesn't bother coming to the door. She and Katie are huddled by the white brick fireplace. Katie waves for me to come over, but because I'm not in the mood to hang with Lenore, I wander to the back, where the kitchen is.

A woman is reaching into the refrigerator. All I can see are her bare feet, sparkly toenail polish and the silver toe ring on one of her baby toes. I can't imagine Lenore having a mom who wears a toe ring, and it turns out I'm right, because when the fridge door closes, I see that the feet belong to Ms. Cameron. Maybe Lenore's parents are out or waiting out the party in one of the rooms upstairs.

"Hey, Ms. Cameron." It feels weird to see your teacher standing in someone's kitchen. "Need some help?"

"That'd be great," she says, handing me a tray of cut-up veggies. "Lenore told me there's some yogurt dip too. If I can find it in here."

"Aha, there you are," she says a moment later, talking to the dip. "Can you grab this too?" She looks at me as if she's just noticed I'm there. "That was a strong performance tonight, Iris. Haunting. You really made us feel how lost and torn you—I mean, Ophelia is. Maybe that extra work Mick's been doing with you has deepened your connection to Ophelia…" She lets her voice trail off.

"I guess," I say, without moving. I don't want to give away too much. I know how good Ms. Cameron is at reading body language.

She touches my elbow. "Look, Iris, I don't like to discuss my personal life with my students." Even though we're the only ones in the kitchen, she lowers her voice. "I was"—she stops to choose her words—"involved…with Mick. We had an argument once and he got a little rough with me. Of course, I broke up with him after that."

It's hard not to react. Mick and Ms. Cameron? How come he never told me they were together? He got *a little rough* with her. And then she broke up with him.

I'm still trying to make sense of what she's just told me, but Ms. Cameron keeps talking.

"I respect his work, but I don't think he has much of a talent for relationships. I heard there was some trouble in Australia too. So, Iris, if you're thinking about getting involved with him, don't! I know how persuasive Mick can be when he wants something. But you're a smart girl, Iris, maybe the smartest I've ever taught. You'll be smart about this too, right?"

"Right," I say as I tuck the tub of dip into the crook of my arm. "And I'm sorry."

"What for?"

How can she not know what I mean? "For what happened. With you and Mick. It must've been awful."

I'm shaking, but I manage somehow to use my other elbow to open the swinging door that leads back out to the main area.

A guy turns around, and as soon as he does, I know it's Errol. I recognize him from the pictures in his bubbie's apartment. What's he doing here?

"Errol!" I say, and without thinking I hand him the tray of veggies.

"Do I know you?" he asks.

"It's me—Iris. Your bubbie's neighbor. I recognize you from the photos in her apartment. What are you doing here?"

"Wow, Iris," he says, extending his free arm to shake mine. "This is pretty weird, isn't it? I came to town to look in on Bubbie, but then I lined up a couple of interviews with some people in McGill's Engineering Department. My friend Tony's younger brother is Vincent, who works sound on the play. Anyway, Vince told us to drop by tonight. Bubbie went to bed early, so I figured I'd hang out here for a bit."

"How'd you like your bubbie's chicken last week?"

Errol grins. "No one makes chicken like my bubbie. Hey," he says, and I catch him looking around the room. "Is your boyfriend here? The older guy?"

"Uh, no, he isn't. He had to work." I drop my voice. "Listen, Errol, if you don't mind, it'd be better if you don't mention him here—or that I even have a boyfriend."

"Okay," he whispers, though I get the feeling it isn't okay and that he wants to say more. Which is why I'm relieved when he asks, "How about I get you another beer?"

I follow Errol to the cooler by the stairway. I can tell from the sweet smoky smell drifting up the stairs that someone is smoking weed in the basement. Errol reaches into the cooler and hands me a beer. He introduces me to a tall guy who wears his hair in a ponytail. Vince's brother, Tony. "That teacher's not with you, is she?" Tony asks.

"You mean Ms. Cameron?" I say. "No, she's in the kitchen, organizing the food."

"Well then, you guys should definitely check out the laundry room in this place," Tony says.

The laundry room is bigger and more tricked out than our kitchen. The washer, dryer and sink are stainless steel; the walls and floors are so white that when I first walk in, my eyes need to adjust to the brightness. But Tony hasn't sent us here for the decor. A bunch of kids are passing around a joint. Katie's with them. She must have come downstairs when I was in the kitchen.

I smoked up a couple of times with Tommy, but it never did anything for me except give me a headache. So when Katie passes me the joint, I hold on to it for a few seconds while I decide whether to take a puff or pass it on. I don't want to end up with another headache, but I also don't want to be the only straight one in the room. Here I go again, unable to make a simple decision. If I can't decide, well then, I probably shouldn't have one. I start to pass the joint to Errol, but at the very last second I take it back and bring it to my lips for a quick puff. I can still see Katie's hot-pink lipstick on the rim. The smoke burns as it travels down my throat and into my lungs.

Maybe this time I do get stoned. Because not too long afterward—how long exactly I'm not sure—I find myself back upstairs, sitting cross-legged on the Persian carpet in Lenore's den. How many fireplaces can one house have? Errol is sitting across from me on an oversized pillow with lots of tassels hanging off it. I'm thinking that if I wasn't going out with Mick, I might think Errol was cute. The thought makes me laugh out loud.

"What's so funny?" Errol wants to know.

"Nothing. It feels like I'm in a play."

"You are in a play, silly," says Lenore, who has wandered into the room. "I'm the leading actress. You've got a small supporting role." She laughs when she says that, then wanders out, like the ghost of Hamlet's father.

Why didn't I notice Ms. Cameron sitting on the couch across from us? I must be really stoned. "We're always in a play. All of us—at every moment," she says, waving her hand in the air. "As the bard says, 'All the world's a stage.' Only in this play, this here-and-now play, there's no rehearsing." She hangs her head as if she thinks that's a bad thing. Then she lifts it to look right at me. "You don't want to make too much of a mess of things, Iris. A little mess is not so bad, but a big mess…" She shakes her head. "A big mess is not so good. It's harder to get out of the big messes. That's why, as Polonius says, we have to tender ourselves more dearly…"

Errol nudges me. "What's she talking about?" he whispers.

"I'm not sure," I whisper back, "but I think I'm stoned." That must have been some strong weed.

"D'you wanna get some fresh air?" Errol asks.

We have to dig to find our jackets on the coatrack. Then we walk along the side of the house to where the back deck is. I hear Errol take a deep breath. "Look Iris, we don't really know each other, and this probably isn't my business. But my bubbie, she's not crazy about your boyfriend. I know she can be a busybody sometimes, but Bubbie's not stupid. She thinks he…well…she thinks maybe he hits you."

For a moment, I am totally sober. Mostly, I think, because I can't believe Errol just said that. "He doesn't," I say. "He wouldn't. Never. Ever. Your bubbie doesn't know him." I say it firmly, so Errol will know he needs to drop the subject. "Besides, I'm a big girl." When I hear myself speak, it sounds like the words are coming from far away, and I realize how stoned I still am. And that I don't want to be having this conversation.

"Look." Errol digs his hands into his jacket pockets. "I'm sorry I said anything. I shouldn't have. It's just…Bubbie worries. Maybe I'm a worrier too. Maybe it's in my genes."

"Did anyone ever hit you?" I ask Errol. I'm not quite sure where the question came from. And it's too late now to take it back.

"My mom once. Not hard though. I was picking on my kid brother. I guess I had it coming." Errol's eyes are blood-shot, and I wonder if that means mine are too. "It was no big deal."

Errol's quiet for a bit. When he speaks again, his voice is thoughtful. "The roughest thing I ever went through was when my zaidie died. I really loved the guy. But even worse than losing him was seeing what happened to my mom. It was the first time I ever saw anybody lose it. Really lose it. When she got the news he was gone, she curled up on the floor and howled like a baby. None of us could make her stop, not even my dad. I'll tell you something, Iris. Seeing her like that, well, it scared me shitless."

CHAPTER 26

"...if like a crab you could go backward."
—*HAMLET*, ACT 2, SCENE 2

Does an image ever just bloom in your head? Like a flower, only without a stem or roots or soil? And nowhere near as pretty as a flower. Not pretty at all—not in my case anyhow.

You don't ask for the picture. It just appears, presto, out of nowhere. And you can't make it go away, even when you try. Once the picture starts to bloom, there's no stopping it.

Maybe it's the weed, but that's what's happening to me now.

The image blooming in my mind is of a girl—a little girl—crouched inside a walk-in closet. She is surrounded by racks of clothing. There are men's clothes on one side, women's on the other. She can tell because the women's clothes feel silky soft; the clothes on the other side are prickly and rough. The smells are different too. The women's clothes smell like lemon, only sweeter; the men's have a warm and spicy smell.

The floor is cold and hard underneath the little girl's legs. Sometimes, as she rocks back and forth, her shoulders touch the crinkly plastic on the clothes that have come from the dry cleaner's. Though I can't yet see the little girl's face, I know it's me. It's as if I can still feel the crinkly plastic on my shoulders and smell the sweet lemon and the warm spices.

In the pictures I've seen of myself when I was little, I'm almost always holding on to a giant blue cloth doll. And smiling. A smile that's too big for my small face.

The little girl in the closet doesn't have her doll—and she isn't smiling.

Something bad is happening, has happened, is about to happen. That's why she's hiding in the closet. It's safer there than out in the living room with them.

"Iris, you okay?" It takes me a moment to reorient myself. Errol's talking to me. We're outside on Lenore's porch, at the cast party. What was it Ms. Cameron said before? *There's no rehearsing.*

"I'm okay. Just a little dizzy. I should probably sit."

"Here, let me help you." Errol leads me to a rattan couch that Lenore's family must have forgotten to take in for the winter. There's a pillow that smells like mould on it. But I need to sit.

Errol helps me. "Is that better?" he asks.

I nod to tell him it is. I want to thank him for being kind to me, but I can't. It's as if the memory is calling me back, asking to be remembered.

Why am I remembering that little girl—me—in the closet? How come when you try hard to remember something—like a joke you heard a long time ago and want to tell your friends—it doesn't always work? And then other times, a memory just comes back, like the image blooming in my head? Why is the little girl so scared?

Part of me is curious and wants to go back and remember; another part doesn't. That other part wants yellow tape around the memory—the sort of tape the police put up after there's been a gruesome accident. The kind that says to everyone who sees it, *Danger! Keep away for your own good!*

But I can't keep away from the yellow tape.

Another picture has begun to bloom.

It's a man—his face is blurry There's a woman now too. Mommy. She's wearing a long yellow sweater dress, and her hair goes past her shoulders. She has an angry face. They are both angry—so angry they have forgotten the little girl who was in the room with them. They didn't even notice when she left to hide in the closet. There wasn't time for her to bring her blue doll.

The little girl presses her hands tight over her ears to block out the angry noises. There, she thinks, that is better.

The picture in my head goes black. Even when I try squinting, the picture won't come back. But there's something else I'm remembering. Not a picture. A sound—the words to an old nursery rhyme.

This little piggy went to market.

This little piggy stayed at home.

And why, now, do I feel a painful throbbing in my ring finger—the little piggy that had none? I haven't done anything to make it sore. I didn't sit on it or bang it into anything.

Errol has gone back inside to get me a glass of water. When he comes back, he says, "Have a drink. It'll make you feel better. That dope was pretty strong, and you got seriously buzzed, Iris. I'm kinda buzzed myself."

"Thanks," I manage to say as I take greedy gulps of the water.

I don't tell Errol about the flashback. I need time to figure out what it means. Besides, I hardly know him.

I look at my fingers holding the water glass. The ring finger, the one that's hurting, is fatter than the rest. It's always been that way. Or has it?

It's the finger that fit my father's ring. He told me the dragon was a symbol of strength. But I took it off after Mick said he didn't like it.

"Are you looking for something?" Errol asks when I pick up my purse from the rattan couch and start rifling through it.

"A ring. From my dad." It's the first time I've used the word *dad,* not *father.*

I have to feel around for the ring, but I finally find it. I blow the lint off it.

I slide the ring back on my finger. This time, I won't take it off. Even if the dragon is creepy. Even if Mick doesn't like it.

CHAPTER 27

"What is between you? Give me up the truth."

—*HAMLET*, ACT 1, SCENE 3

It's nearly 2:00 AM when Errol drops me off at Mom's. Thank God her bedroom light is off. I let myself in as quietly as I can. But then I hear her trudging down the stairs. Even in the dark, I can feel her standing in the hall. "I know we said we'd talk tomorrow, Iris," she says. At least she didn't call me *Iris Wagner.* Maybe she's just glad I'm home.

"Mom, I'm going straight to bed."

"I just wanted to know you were safe."

I let her rock me in her arms for a few seconds before I pull away. "I'm safe, Mom," I whisper into the darkness.

I almost text Mick when I get into bed. But I'm afraid to wake him. And if he isn't at the loft…well, I don't want to know.

⁓

In the morning, everything's the same. Mom and I sit at our usual table at the front of the bagel place. We have our usual breakfast: toasted sesame bagels with scrambled eggs (I wasn't in the mood for poached), fruit salad instead of potatoes. We even have the same waitress. I help her with the cutlery.

Yet everything is different.

Somehow, I managed to sleep last night, even though my head was spinning from trying to figure things out. How much can I tell my mom about what's going on? And why did I remember hiding in the closet? I want to ask her about that, but I'm not sure I can. And what about my father? Will I have the courage to talk to her about him?

It's hard to know where to begin the conversation. Mostly because my mom and I don't usually have these kinds of conversations.

Mom doesn't know how to begin this conversation either. "You're too thin," she says. "Maybe you should have ordered the potatoes."

I pop a pale green cube of honeydew melon into my mouth. "The fruit salad tastes funny. Like it's been sitting around too long."

Mom tries the fruit salad. She wrinkles her nose. "I know what you mean. Let's send it back."

"We never send anything back. We only talk about it."

Mom uses the back of her fork to push the rest of her fruit salad to the side of her plate. Then she clears her throat. She's working her way up to what she's brought me here to discuss. "Iris, the first thing I want to say is, I'm not angry with you. I'm disappointed—deeply disappointed, because I thought we had a better relationship than this—but I'm not angry, Iris." The way she keeps saying she isn't angry only confirms that she is.

I am wringing my paper napkin under the table. I'm sorry about disappointing her and making her angry, even if she says she isn't.

If she realized last night that I might be angry too—and I think she did—she seems to have decided not to mention it. I'm more and more aware that not mentioning things is how Mom operates. Maybe she stuffs the things she doesn't want to face into some closet in her brain.

"Maybe it's my fault," she goes on. "Maybe I haven't made you feel you could be honest with me."

"It's not that. You've been fine. You've been great. Always." When I say the words, I realize I'm doing what my mom does—smoothing things over, protecting someone else's feelings. I don't want her thinking she's been a bad mother.

Mom has put down her fork and is gripping the edge of the table with both hands. "So what the fuck is going on then, Iris?"

I nearly drop my fork. I can't believe Mom just said "fuck." She never says "fuck." She never even says "damn."

Mom catches my reaction. "What do you think?" she asks me. "That I never swear?"

"If you did, I never heard you."

"I've always done my best to set a good example, Iris. I've tried to create an environment where you could be honest with me. But now I know that hasn't worked." Mom shakes her head. It's hard to know if she's more disappointed in me or in herself.

"Like I told you last night, there's kind of a lot of stuff going on," I say. "It's hard for me to talk about."

Mom sighs. She's not going to let me get away with not telling her what's been going on. "Let's start by talking about where you've been staying. When you haven't been staying at Katie's. I take it there's a boy involved."

"It's not a boy."

Mom looks at me really hard. "You're gay?"

That makes me laugh. Maybe I also laugh because I'm tense from holding so much in. "It's a man. Not a boy."

"A man?"

"Try not to shout, Mom. We're in a public place."

"How old is this man exactly, Iris?"

"He's thirty-one."

"Thirty-one?" The color drains out of Mom's face. "My God, Iris, are you insane? This…this man is more than a decade older than you are."

I understand Mom is upset that I've been keeping something like this from her, and that Mick is fourteen years older than me. But for the first time I wonder if maybe she is jealous. She's always said she didn't have time for a boyfriend. Not between raising me and running her business.

"That's why I didn't tell you. I knew you'd freak out. But Mom, what you need to understand is…we really love each other. And you can't talk me out of it."

Mom shakes her head. "A fourteen-year age difference— at your age—well, it's huge. It's practically a lifetime. You're still a child, Iris."

"No, I'm not. And you have to stop treating me like one."

Mom is not listening. "How did you meet this man anyhow?"

"Through theater." I can feel the words sitting in the air between us.

"I see." She adjusts her knees as if that will make it easier for her to say what she wants to say next. "Unfortunately, I know exactly what a man of thirty-one would want with a seventeen-year-old."

"You don't understand. The age difference doesn't mean anything to me." I correct myself. "To us."

"Well, I'll tell you one thing, Iris: seventeen-year-olds don't know the first thing about life—or relationships."

"That isn't true. I know something about life." I'm trying to make her understand what it is I know. "I'm learning," I say. It's the best I can come up with.

Mom nods. It's more a giving-up than an agreeing-with nod. "Well then, all I can say is, that I want to meet this *man*friend of yours. As soon as possible."

I don't have the heart to tell her she's already met him.

So I don't say anything. Instead, I run my fingertip over my plate to pick up the last few sesame seeds. That's when Mom notices my dragon ring. "That ring," she says. "Is it from him?"

I shake my head. I'm tired of telling lies. I'm tired of keeping track of the lies I've already told.

I've been looking for a way to talk to her about my father—my dad. "You know what you said before about seventeen-year-olds not knowing anything about relationships? Were you remembering when you were this age?"

Mom rubs her forehead. I don't want her to start feeling sick, but I can't keep waiting for a better time to have this conversation.

"Weren't you seventeen when you met my father?"

"That isn't what I meant." Mom hasn't answered my questions. I can't see her hands. Is she playing with her napkin now?

"I was at this party last night and I..." I have to be careful not to tell Mom too much about the party. She'd freak out about the weed. Mom thinks smoking up once means you're headed straight for crack addiction. "I started remembering something that happened...a really long time ago. When my father was still around."

Mom crosses her arms across her chest.

"I remembered hiding in a closet."

Mom shuts her eyes, then opens them again. She reaches across the table for my hand. I let her take it. I wonder if she's always noticed that one of my fingers is fatter than the rest. "Oh Iris," she whispers. "I always hoped you wouldn't remember. You were so little when he left."

These are always the words Mom uses when she talks about my father. That he left us. But now I understand that that may not be how it really went. "You kicked him out, didn't you? You made him go."

Mom nods but doesn't volunteer any more information.

"What did he do that was so bad?" I can almost feel the floor shift under me. It's the question I've never dared ask her.

"I didn't have a choice," Mom says. "He nearly ruined us." Mom's voice is so quiet, it's hard for me to hear her over the buzz of conversation around us. "I've told you before he had terrible problems with money..."

Mom's voice catches in her throat, and I know she doesn't want to tell me more.

But I need to know. Even if it's hard for her. "But what did he do exactly?" I ask, prompting her. "Max out your credit cards?" In Economics, the teacher warned us about the dangers of credit-card debt and how even before we graduate from university, credit-card companies will be fighting for our business.

Mom bites her lip. Whatever happened was worse than credit-card debt.

The waitress offers to refill our coffee. Mom wants more. She takes forever to peel the cover from the little plastic cream container. Then she stirs the coffee, first in one direction, then the other. She looks at me. "Maybe the reason you've fallen for some inappropriate older man is because your father's out of the picture."

"M—" I stop myself just in time from saying Mick's name. "He isn't inappropriate." I must be raising my voice, because a man at the next table turns to look at me. "Did you ever think that not telling me about my dad...well, maybe that wasn't the best idea? Maybe there were too many secrets in our house. Too many things we could never talk about. So he lost a lot of money. Our money. It's not the end of the world. We got through it."

"It wasn't just our money," Mom whispers.

I don't know what she means. "Whose money was it?"

"Lots of people's money. My parents' money. The neighbors who lived on our street, people we'd gone to school with…pretty much everyone we knew. Yes, your father had credit-card debt, but that was the least of it. That we could have dealt with. But there was more—your father talked other people into investing their money with him. He lost nearly three million dollars—of other people's money." I picture my father's smile when she says that. The kind of smile that would make people like him, trust him. "Some of that money went into bad investments." Mom stops to take a breath. I can tell it's hard for her to go on, but she does. "He gambled the rest of it away. At high-stakes private card games, at the casino. He kept promising me he'd stop the gambling, that he'd get professional help, but he never did. He was addicted to the thrill. I couldn't live with that."

"He gambled away three million dollars?" It's such a large amount, I can't get my mind around it. "Is that why he's not allowed in the country?"

Mom nods. "That and the fact that he still owes a fortune to Revenue Canada. At least they didn't come after us for that."

"Mom," I say, looking right at her. I swallow hard. "I saw him."

"Saw who?"

"Him. My father. My dad."

Mom rubs her belly with both hands. How could her stomach be hurting so soon?

"What are you talking about, Iris?"

"We've been in touch. On Facebook and over the telephone. We met up in Plattsburgh. In October."

"In October?" Mom's voice breaks. "And you didn't tell me?"

"He gave me the ring." I extend my arm so she can see the ring. But she won't look at it.

"How could you not have told me, Iris?"

"I'm telling you now."

"How is he?"

It's the last question I expect from her.

"He's okay, I guess. He's working on some big deal."

"He always was." She says it sadly.

"Did you love him?" I don't know why I never thought of asking her this question before. Because now it seems to me like the most important question in the world. The only question.

Mom doesn't say she loved him. Or that she didn't love him.

All she says is this: "I had to make myself stop."

"Stop what?"

Mom looks down at her hands as if they might have the answer. "Stop loving him. It was the hardest thing I ever had to do."

I could feel sorry for her, but I don't. I don't even care that I've hurt her. She's hurt me, too, by keeping my father away from me all these years. Even if he did bad things, reckless things, he was still my father. She could have let me speak to him; when I was older, she could have found a way to let me meet him.

"He told me he tried to stay in touch. But that you blocked him. That you changed our number. He said I should ask you why you did it."

Mom's face is crumbling. "I'm sorry," she says. "I didn't know what else to do. I was protecting you..."

"Protecting me?"

We both know it's a lie. She was protecting herself.

Mom sighs. "I was afraid"—now I notice that her upper lip is trembling—"afraid I wouldn't be able to live without him. That if I saw him again, or even heard his voice, I'd give in..."

~

I don't see Mick all weekend. He texts to tell me it's better this way. All I know is life feels flat and dull when I'm not with him. I've gotten so used to thinking of myself as part of a couple ("me and Mick") that I'm not sure anymore who *me* is without him. At least Mom doesn't bombard me with more questions. Either she's making so much it hurts

a big effort not to be annoying or she's recovering from
our talk at the bagel place. Maybe a combination of
the two.

I spend Saturday and Sunday afternoons studying
in my room. Concentrating, which usually comes easily
to me, feels like a huge effort. But when I'm finally able
to focus on economics or world history, I forget—for a
while anyhow—what a terrible mess I've made of things.

Mom stands outside the door a lot, asking if I want
green tea. "No sugar. Not too strong. Just the way you like
it." In the end, I say yes to the tea, more to make her go
away than anything. Why is it that love can sometimes
feel like a burden?

It seems like forever till it's finally Monday after
school. When I let myself into the loft, Mick is already
there. The place looks brighter and shinier than usual.
Mick must've cleaned over the weekend. Maybe because
he was so lonely for me. Maybe because he feels bad that
I've been doing so much of the housework.

Mick meets me in the doorway. William Shakespeare
comes too, and I lean down to pet him. When I straighten,
Mick scoops me into his arms and dances me to the table.
I'm breathless and giggling. He's chilled a bottle of his
favorite Australian chardonnay; he's even chilled our
wineglasses. When I reach for my glass, my fingers leave
their prints on the frosted surface.

That's when Mick notices the dragon ring. "I thought you didn't like that ring," he says.

"You're the one who didn't like it," I tell him. "I'm hoping it'll make me stronger."

"You're strong enough already." Mick looks so deep into my eyes that I almost have to look away. "Let's toast, Joey, to our new beginning. Oh God, I've missed you the last few days. I'm aching for you."

I love it when he tells me that. "Me too," I say. "Aching." We clink glasses. "To our new beginning." I have the same feeling I had the day Mick and I had our first real conversation—over lattes on Mount Royal Avenue—the feeling that he really *gets* me. He must know how much I want a new beginning. How much I need a new beginning. There's so much I want to tell him...all the things I've been thinking about over the weekend. I need to tell him about the memory that came back at the cast party and about the things I've learned about my father—and my mother.

Mick breaks into a huge smile. I don't think I've ever seen him look so happy. I know it's because he's been aching to see me and now the ache is over. "I've taken a job in Melbourne!" he says.

It's as if all the air's been sucked out of the apartment. "You did what?"

"Don't look so surprised, Joey. It's a fantastic offer from the Melbourne Theater Company, which is a very prestigious place. You must have realized this could happen." Mick is still smiling. "Of course, I want you to come, Joey, so you can get to know Nial."

I'm so surprised that at first, I can't even make words. "But...what about William Shakespeare?" I finally sputter. It's a weird question, but it's the first one that pops into my head.

"We'll give him away," Mick says, sweeping his hand through the air as if the problem of William Shakespeare is already solved.

"Give him away? Can't he come with us?"

"Things like that can be complicated. There's all kinds of paperwork involved."

William Shakespeare is sitting on my feet, oblivious to the fact that his future is up for discussion. I pick him up and hold him close to my chest. His back paws dangle down against my belly. "I can't give him away."

"We'll see what we can do, Joey. He is just a cat."

"He's *our* cat."

"The more important question, Joey, is what you're going to do in Melbourne. It's just like you to put the damn cat before yourself." Mick shakes his head, and immediately I'm sorry for upsetting him. "I did some research over the weekend. There's still time for you to apply to some very prestigious theater programs in Melbourne."

I wish Mick didn't use the word *prestigious* so much.

That's when I realize Mick hasn't even asked me whether I *want* to go to Melbourne. He just assumes I'll follow him. He's right, of course, and we both know it. Which is why he didn't ask. I'd follow him anywhere. That's what love is, isn't it? But at this very second, I feel dizzy, and I don't think it's because I've had a few sips of chardonnay. It's the idea of moving so far away and of not having anyone there I know besides Mick. What will my mom do without me? She'll freak out when I tell her.

"I really want to get to know Nial." I'm picturing Mick and me and Nial together, having a picnic in Melbourne. The three of us are sitting on a blanket, and Nial is laughing so hard he throws his head back. And I know Mick will be happier and less tense when he's not so far away from his son. He won't lose his temper the way he has here in Montreal.

"He's going to love you," Mick says. "Just like his dad does."

How is it that when Mick wants to, he always seems to know the exact right thing to say?

We have sex. Twice. Maybe when we're in Melbourne together, I'll be able to relax more during sex. Mick says he can't get enough of me and that no one else—no one—has ever made him feel this way. That makes me think of the poem I found, but I don't bring it up again.

Afterward, when I'm curled around him, I tell Mick about the memory that came back. His spine tenses up, but he doesn't say anything. I hope I haven't upset him.

"What about you, Mick? Did bad things ever happen to you when you were little?" I whisper into his back. I'm glad I don't have to see his face.

Mick's spine tenses up again. Then he takes a long deep breath, and I know he's thinking about my question.

"Did anyone ever hurt you, Mick?"

I know it's a terrible question, but I have to ask it. Even if I already know the answer. Of course someone hurt him. That's why Mick thinks it's okay to hurt me. Maybe talking things out will bring us even closer. But Mick doesn't want to talk things out. "The past is the past, Joey," is all he'll say.

Later, I get on the computer and start checking out the theater programs offered in Melbourne.

Part of me is scared silly. Melbourne?

Another part of me is crazy excited. Moving to Melbourne will mean starting a brand-new life. A clean slate. When I think about my life, a clean slate is exactly what I need.

CHAPTER 28

"What dreams may come...
Must give us pause." —HAMLET, ACT 3, SCENE 1

To go or not to go to Melbourne? That is my question.

I'm lying in my narrow bed, trying to imagine my future. I can feel myself getting sleepy—my arms and legs are heavy, my breaths are longer, and I'm not so anxious anymore. When I close my eyes, I don't see any too-tall trees. Instead, I see Mick and me.

It's as if I'm watching a play inside my head, with the two of us co-starring. I feel my lips curling into a smile. Mick and I look so good together.

I'm going with him to Melbourne. We'll have two stopovers—one in Vancouver and another in Honolulu. I love the sound of the word Honolulu. Just saying it makes me happy.

I ask Mick whether we can extend the Honolulu stopover so that we can have a beach weekend, but he says no way.

Too expensive, and we need to watch our money. He says he doesn't understand how I can be thinking about holiday weekends when we have so much to get organized.

Mick and I have two suitcases each. Plus we've sent some things—like books and winter clothes—by cargo. I've brought a whole bunch of picture books for Nial. All the ones I used to love when I was little. Good Night Moon *and* One Fish, Two Fish. *One of the things I like imagining is how I'll read to him before he goes to bed, the way Mom used to do with me. Mick thinks Nial will spend a couple of nights every week with us and alternate weekends too. Mick and Nial and I will be our own little family. In a few years, once I've finished theater school and got my career established, Mick and I might even have a baby of our own.*

We're sitting at the airport gate when there's an announcement that the flight to Vancouver is going to be delayed. The airplane hasn't yet arrived in Montreal. Mick scowls when he checks the time on his cell phone. "It's not going to be easy to make the first connecting flight," he says, his voice tight.

"I guess there's nothing we can do about it." I reach for his hand, but he doesn't give it to me. Instead, he gives me an irritated look, as if I'm the one responsible for delaying the flight. I haven't said so, but I think Mick is nervous about going back to Melbourne and having to juggle even more things than he's had to juggle here in Montreal—work, Nial, Nial's mom and the lawyer, and now, of course, he'll also have to look after me, make sure I'm adjusting to life far away from home.

"You know what I've noticed about this airline?" a woman sitting across from us says to no one in particular. "They tell you it's going to be a one-hour delay, and then an hour later, they tell you there's been another delay. You know what I wish?" The woman doesn't wait for anyone to ask her what it is she wishes. "I wish these big corporations would just give it to us straight in the first place."

"I'm with you," Mick tells the woman.

I fight the urge to say, You're with me, not her. What good would saying it do? Besides, it would sound like I'm jealous, which I'm not.

The woman turns out to be right. Exactly one hour later, there's another announcement: the flight from Vancouver won't be arriving for at least another hour. There's been engine trouble.

"Goddammit," Mick mutters under his breath.

I stroke the top of his hand. The blue veins look like rivers on a topographical map. "There's nothing we can do," I whisper.

Mick pulls his hand away. "For God's sake, will you stop saying that?" He is raising his voice now. It's one thing for him to shout at me in the loft, but this is the first time he's shouted at me when other people are around. I can feel the woman across from us watching.

"Please don't shout." I'm trying not to cry.

Mick's eyes have that angry, unhinged flash they get just before he loses it. He takes my hand, and for a second I'm confused. Why does Mick want to hold hands now? I feel that old familiar hope building inside me. Maybe this time Mick will be different. Maybe this time he'll catch himself and be calm and kind, not angry. Maybe. Please.

But I'm wrong. Mick doesn't want to hold my hand. Instead, he uses his fingers like a vice, pressing down hard— too hard—on both sides of my hand. I swear I hear the bones crack. He's pressing down too hard for me to pull away.

"Stop it," I whisper—I really don't want anyone to hear— but he won't.

It's only when my eyes fill with tears that Mick finally lets go. I blink back the tears.

The woman is still watching. Judging Mick and me. Disapproving. I pass her when I get up from my seat to go to the bathroom. "Your boyfriend sure seems to be a nasty piece of work," she whispers. "What are you doing with him?"

In the bathroom, I splash my face with cold water. I can still feel Mick's fingers crushing my hand.

He's stressed out about making our connection in Vancouver. He's stressed out about the long trip ahead. He's stressed out about seeing Nial and dealing with Millicent and the lawyer. He'll be better in Melbourne. I shouldn't have told him there was nothing we could do about the delay. I should've known better. I should've been watching for land mines.

I take the long way back to my seat so I don't have to pass the woman who made the mean comment about Mick. What does she know? She's probably jealous because she's traveling alone.

I'll bet she wishes she had a hot boyfriend. She's bitter. I can hear it in her voice, see it in her face.

Mick smiles at me when I sit down. There's no more angry flash in his eyes. "Good news," he says. "I spoke to an attendant. The plane to Vancouver'll be here in twenty minutes. They're going to hold the next plane—the one to Honolulu. So we're going to be fine, Joey."

"That's good. That's great." I let him kiss me.

More than anything in the world, I need for us to be fine. In Melbourne, Mick will be all I've got.

He reaches into his jeans pocket. I'm sure he's going to offer me a piece of gum or candy. Instead, he fishes out a gold pocket watch. It's one of those really old-fashioned ones with a thin gold chain. Mick's long fingers work quickly as he winds the watch by hand. "I'm going to set it on Melbourne time," he says. "Pretty, isn't it? I picked it up for Nial." Mick turns the watch around and shows me the N engraved in cursive on the back of the watch.

Oh my god. I've seen that watch before. It was Nelson Karpman's.

"That watch!"

My own voice wakes me up.

Where am I? What's going on? We have a plane to catch…but no, I'm in my own bedroom.

"Iris? Is everything okay up there?" Mom calls from the kitchen.

I sit up in my bed. "I'm fine," I call back. "It was just a dream."

Just a dream. But so real that I need to shake out my fingers—the ones I imagined Mick crushing. What an awful dream!

Thank goodness that was all it was. An awful, silly dream. Mick would never hurt me in front of other people. And he'd never steal Nelson Karpman's watch.

CHAPTER 29

"More matter, with less art."
—HAMLET, ACT 2, SCENE 2

We're at the loft, packing.

I've applied to two theater schools in Melbourne and have already had an early acceptance from one, but I still haven't decided for sure to follow Mick to Australia. It's the worst case of indecision I've ever had. A zillion times worse than when I was a little girl choosing ice cream. The thing is, I can't imagine living without Mick. But I also can't imagine living in Australia. I have the terrible feeling that whatever I end up deciding will be wrong. So for now, I've decided not to decide. I'm just trying to live inside that fuzzy, unsettling place that for me is Indecision.

Mick is sending his books by cargo. The Australian theater company will cover the cost of the move, including shipping. They've even agreed to pay for shipping my stuff too, if, in the end, I decide to go to Melbourne with Mick.

He's taking two suitcases and a carry-on bag. "Have you seen my passport?" Mick looks relieved when I know exactly where it is—in the pile of things where I found the legal papers and the poem. The one he said he'd written for me.

"That has to go in my carry-on," Mick says when I show him I've found the passport. "I'll do it."

I've already reached for Mick's carry-on bag. It's made of soft tan leather, and it feels expensive.

I unzip the bag. Which is when I spot the gold pocket watch with the gold chain so delicate a spider might have spun it. It's right there, in the silky side pocket. I can't help sucking in my breath. The back of the pocket watch has a curly *N* engraved on it. I'd know that watch anywhere. It was Nelson Karpman's.

Just like in my dream. Could I be dreaming again? I pinch my arm, but no, this is real.

I pull the watch out of the bag. "What are you doing with this?" My voice sounds stronger than I'm used to hearing it. I think because this isn't about me—it's about my friend. That watch belongs to Mrs. Karpman.

"What do you mean *what am I doing with this?* It's an antique pocket watch. I bought it at an antique shop on Notre-Dame Street. For Nial. Did you notice the

N on the back?" Mick is talking more quickly than usual, but he's looking at me. Most liars can't make eye contact when they're lying. Unless, of course, they're actors—or theater directors with a background in acting. I'm sure Mick is lying. I'd recognize that pocket watch anywhere.

I'm shaking. Not because I'm afraid, the way I usually am when I start shaking; it's because I'm angry. White-hot burning angry.

"It's Mrs. Karpman's watch!" I don't care if I'm shouting. I don't care if the whole world hears. "It belonged to her husband. I know because I saw it in a photo. You stole it, didn't you? You took the key she gave me and broke into her apartment!" I'm too angry to cry.

"Of course not. Why would I rob a helpless old woman?"

At first, Mick's question throws me. Why *would* he rob a helpless old woman? Why would he rob my friend? Because, in some strange way, Mrs. Karpman has become the best friend I have. And then the answer comes to me. He'd rob her because he *could*—and because she is my closest friend right now. Mick has been trying to take everything away from me—even my friends. The worst part is *I've let him.* I've let him rob Mrs. Karpman. I've let him take everything away from me—or almost everything.

"How could you do this to her? To me?"

Mick won't answer.

I'm dangling the watch in the air in front of him. Now I hold it to my chest. "I'm bringing it back to her. Now."

Mick blocks my way. "Iris, don't be ridiculous." He makes it sound like this is no big deal, that he just happens to have Mrs. Karpman's husband's watch. That he didn't just lie to me about buying it at some antique store. *On Notre-Dame Street.*

"If you bring it back to her, she'll know who robbed her apartment." Mick keeps his voice low, as if he's afraid the walls will hear. "I could go to jail. And so could you. You gave me the key, remember?"

"I never gave you the key and you know it! You took it from the drawer!"

Mick shakes his head, and for a moment, I doubt myself. "Next you'll be saying you didn't steal those clothes from Forever 21 either," he says.

"I didn't," I sputter. "You made me do it. You forced me to." Even to my own ears, the words sound hollow— because I don't really believe them. I could have said no. To the stealing. To everything. Just like I could have left the first time Mick hit me. Ms. Cameron didn't stick around after Mick became violent. Or I could have left before that—when he punched a hole in the wall. But I didn't. Doesn't that make me almost as much to blame as him?

Everyone knows about women who stay in unhealthy relationships. In abusive relationships even. But they don't get good grades in school or have families who love them. I can't be one of those women.

Or can I?

I could cry. I could drop down on my knees right now and weep and weep and never stop. Because I'm trapped and lost, with no place to go. Just like in my dream.

I can't go back to Mom's. I don't belong there anymore. Not in my single bed with her patrolling outside my door, offering me green tea.

I can't stay here. Once Mick leaves, I could never afford this place on my own.

I can't go to Mrs. Karpman's. Because as angry as I am with Mick, I don't want him to go to jail.

And I don't want to go to Australia. At least, not now.

I've got no place to go.

I'm as badly off as Ophelia—and look what she did. She killed herself. I picture that now too. Where would I even go to drown myself? I'd have to jump from the Jacques-Cartier or Champlain Bridge if I wanted to drown in the St. Lawrence River. I could never do that. I suppose I could just walk into the water the way Virginia Woolf did when she killed herself. Or I could take a whole bottle of pain pills. Katie's dad takes them for his back; I've seen them in their bathroom cupboard. I could steal the bottle—the way I stole those clothes at Forever 21. The memory makes me feel even more miserable.

Or I could jump in front of the metro and give Katie something to talk about.

I've made such a mess of things.

How will I ever make things better? How will I ever find a way to clean up the terrible mess I've made?

Tender yourself more dearly.

Why am I quoting Polonius? And now I remember that that's also what Ms. Cameron was trying to tell me at the cast party.

She said, *We have to tender ourselves more dearly.*

Polonius was criticizing Ophelia for having given herself away too easily to Hamlet. He was telling her she should have valued herself more. Is it possible I've made the same mistake? That I haven't valued myself enough? Given my heart away too easily the way she did with Hamlet?

And now I begin to see another layer to the words. *Tender* has another, gentler meaning that has nothing to do with value or money. Maybe I need to be more tender with myself. Gentler. Look after myself better.

"Pull yourself together, Iris." Mick is breathing hard and moving toward me. But his eyes aren't flashing the way they do when he's about to hit me. There's a look I'm not used to seeing in his dark eyes. Fear. Mick is afraid I'll tell people what he did. What we both did. Realizing that gives me courage I didn't know I had.

"You lied to me. About Mrs. Karpman. Just like you lied to me about that poem. The one you said you wrote for me."

Mick opens his arms, and when he speaks, his voice sounds like a lullaby. "Come here, Joey. I can explain everything."

I could snuggle in his arms. I could let him try to explain what he is doing with Nelson Karpman's watch. I could hope for another new beginning, the way I always do with Mick.

Or I could try to leave. Try, because I'm not sure I can do it and because I know it will be hard. Despite everything that's happened, Mick still has a hold over me. But I've discovered something else: I'm going to have to tender myself more dearly. Even if Ophelia couldn't do it, I think I can.

"I'm keeping the watch," I tell Mick. "I'll think of something to tell Mrs. Karpman."

I half expect Mick to grab the watch from my hands. But he doesn't. Instead, he zips up his leather carry-on bag. "Fine," he says. "Have it your way."

CHAPTER 30

"This above all: to thine own self be true,
And it must follow, as the night the day..."
—*HAMLET*, ACT 1, SCENE 3

I gave Mick another chance. He went down on his knees and swore to me that he bought the watch at an antique store on Notre-Dame Street. He said he'd even take me there to prove it. When I said he didn't have to, he took the watch back to Mrs. Karpman himself—and explained how he got it. How whoever stole it must have sold it to the shop.

Mick left for Melbourne on Friday. We said our good-byes in the loft. I knew I'd lose it if I went downstairs and watched him step into the taxi. When I started to cry, Mick kissed my tears away. He cried too. He told me we had to be brave, that we'd be together soon. He said he wanted me to come the minute exams are over in June. He said he'd pay for the trip. He promised he'd never hurt me again—ever.

And, for the first time, Mick apologized. "I haven't been the best man I could be," he said, "but I'm going to do better. I'm going to work to deserve you, Joey."

Because Mick had to pay the rent until the end of May, he said I should use the loft. Mom was against the idea until I told her I'd get more studying done. "Besides," I added, "it might help me clear my head."

She liked that part too.

Only I haven't been doing much studying—or clearing my head. Unless bawling counts as a way to clear your head. I didn't know a person could cry so many tears. Not even William Shakespeare—the cat or the playwright—can cheer me up.

Now Mrs. Karpman is at the door. "Even with two bad ears, I can hear you wailing, Iris. I've listened to it nonstop since he left and now, well, enough is enough." She reaches out with her arm, and for a moment, I think she wants to shake me. I'm relieved when she lets her arm drop back to her side.

"How long did you cry after Nelson died?"

"A long time. But that was different. Nelson was different. Anyway, I'm an old woman and I didn't come here to argue, Iris. I came to invite you for tea."

I can't stay upset with Mrs. Karpman. "I have a better idea. Why don't you have tea here?"

It's Mrs. Karpman's first time inside the loft. "I think he likes me," she says when William Shakespeare brushes up against her. "Maybe he smells canary."

Mrs. Karpman has never tried herbal tea. I tell her chamomile is supposed to be relaxing. "Red Rose relaxes me just fine," she says, but when she tries the chamomile, she says she likes it.

"You get used to it," she says. At first, I think she means chamomile tea, but then I realize she is talking about Mick's being gone.

"I haven't told you yet," I tell her, "but I'm going to Melbourne. To be with him—and to go to theater school. I'm leaving as soon as my last exam is over in June."

Mrs. Karpman nearly spills her chamomile tea. "I think that's an awful idea, Iris. Imagine following some man to the other end of the earth. Especially a man who's as temperamental as that Aussie." When Mrs. Karpman calls Mick *temperamental*, I know it's because of what she suspects. "Above everything else," she adds, "a woman needs to be independent."

I can't believe it when she says that! "You weren't independent. And look how well it worked out for you."

"That's beside the point. Those were different days, Iris. Few women earned their own livings. We depended on our husbands to support us. If you had a bad husband—one who cheated or beat you"—she watches my face, but I'm careful not to react—"there wasn't much you could do about it. I was lucky with Nelson. But I'm independent now and I'm enjoying it, thank you very much. Nowadays women can do anything they want. To be honest, Iris, I still don't trust that fellow of yours. He's too smooth, and I know he loses his temper, even if you won't admit it." She gives me a sharp look. "To me—or to yourself."

I'm proud for standing up to her. "You can't keep saying bad things about Mick. I love him and that's that. If you want to stay my friend, you'll have to accept that and support my decision."

When she nods, I know I've won my case. "Will you at least promise to send me postcards—and to visit whenever you're back in Montreal? To be honest, I did hope you and Errol might—"

I cut Mrs. Karpman off before she can finish her sentence. "I promise."

Mrs. Karpman takes another sip of chamomile tea. "So is he there yet—in Australia?" she asks.

"He was supposed to arrive last night. Our time, that is."

"I suppose he's been on the phone with you, acting all lovey-dovey, hasn't he?"

I give Mrs. Karpman my bravest smile. I don't want to admit that since he left I haven't heard a word from Mick.

I serve Mrs. Karpman store-bought chocolate-chip cookies. Before she goes, she pats me on the cheek. "I know it hurts to be alone, dear. But you're a courageous girl."

"Do you really think so?"

"Of course I do. It's one of the reasons I like you so much."

~

I text Mick, but he doesn't text me back. I know his plane arrived on time because I followed his flights online. It's a long trip, so maybe he went straight to bed. He'll text or phone me when he wakes up.

I don't feel like studying, but when I finally get down to it, it helps. When I can't read any more about gross national product and how it's calculated, I take a break to look at theater programs in Melbourne.

There's a school called the Victorian College of the Arts. It's part of the University of Melbourne, and it offers a bachelor's degree in theater arts. I click on the link for the program. There's a video ad. In it, I see short clips of students doing warm-up exercises like the ones Ms. Cameron uses, and other clips from theatrical performances. Some of the students are doing mime. Others are in musicals. One is of a choreographed fight between a guy and a girl.

The girl is Millicent Temple.

I watch the video five times. Either Millicent is a very good actor or she's had experience fighting.

It's impossible to study after that. I keep thinking about Millicent. Did she love Mick as much as I do? No, I think, she couldn't have. No one could love Mick as much as I do.

My phone rings. It's my mom—not Mick. I try not to sound disappointed. She says she's nearby and she's picked up a vegetarian pizza. "I'd like to come and see the loft," she says. After our conversation about my dad, I ended up telling her that Mick is my boyfriend. She didn't take it well. Still, I can tell she's trying, even though it must be hard for her.

I'm so used to hiding out, I nearly say no. Then I realize that with Mick gone, I can have anyone I want over. And it's not as if I'm nursing a black eye. "Okay," I tell her. "It's apartment nine-oh-seven."

"By the way, Iris," Mom says, "I'm not alone." She hangs up before I can ask who is with her.

CHAPTER 31

"...to know a man well were to know himself."
—*HAMLET*, ACT 5, SCENE 2

I hear more than two pairs of high heels clicking down the corridor. Maybe more than three pairs.

I expect to see Mom when I open the door. But first I see Katie. Mom is behind her. With Ms. Cameron and Ms. Odette. And why is Tommy marching down the hallway, carrying the pizza cartons?

William Shakespeare has come to the door with me. When he sees the crowd of people, he meows and races back inside, probably to hide underneath the couch.

I want to slam the door in their faces. "What's going on?" I ask instead.

"We brought pizza," Mom announces.

Tommy is the only one who has the decency to look embarrassed.

"Mom, can I talk to you—privately?"

The others take a few steps back. I hear shuffling sounds in Mrs. Karpman's apartment. Now she's cracking open her door to see what's going on. "Has everyone arrived?" she asks.

I get so close to my mom, our faces nearly touch. "You didn't say you were bringing all those people," I hiss.

"Iris," she says grimly, "this is an intervention. You're going to have to let us in."

The intervention turns out to be Mrs. Karpman's idea. "How did you even know what an intervention was?" I ask as she bustles past me.

"Errol told me about it," she says. "He thought it might be a good idea."

"Listen, all of you," I say while they are filing into the apartment, "I don't mind having you here for pizza, but I don't need an intervention."

"Interventions are for people who don't think they need interventions," Katie says. From her tone, you'd think she participates in interventions regularly.

Tommy heads for the kitchen, where he begins opening the pizza cartons. Seeing Tommy in Mick's loft feels wrong. "Are there napkins here somewhere?" he calls.

Mom takes my hand and leads me to the couch as if I'm a blind person. "I know this must feel overwhelming, Iris, but you have to understand that it's for your own good."

Ms. Odette plops down next to me. "I should explain, Iris," she says, giving me a tight-lipped smile, "that typically, interventions are used to assist individuals struggling with substance abuse." Doesn't she realize she sounds like one of her brochures? "Of course, we know that isn't exactly your case, dear."

"You're right. I'm not an addict—and don't call me *dear*."

Ms. Odette nods. "It's perfectly normal for you to feel angry right now," she says. At least she doesn't call me *dear* again.

Katie helps Tommy hand out pizza slices and napkins.

Ms. Cameron is poking around the apartment as if she has a right to. "Don't touch that!" I tell her when she stops to examine the print of the Bonsecours Market. Someone must have brushed against it, because it isn't hanging straight. I can tell Ms. Cameron wants to adjust it. I shouldn't have said anything. Ms. Cameron curls her lip, then turns back to the print. She moves the edge of the frame, gasping when she sees what's behind it.

Everyone turns to see what's happened. Ms. Cameron lifts the print off the wall and exposes the hole underneath. It's so obviously shaped like a fist that for once I don't try coming up with a story to cover for Mick.

"Oh my god," Katie says.

Ms. Odette puts her hand on Katie's elbow. "It's important that we all stay calm," she tells her.

I wonder if they've scripted this intervention. Everyone seems to have something to say to me. It reminds me of a fairytale I loved when I was little. Five fairies come to bestow their wishes on a newborn princess. Only I've got six fairies, one's a guy, and they're all eating pizza and annoying the hell out of me.

Ms. Cameron goes first. She's still holding the print on her lap. "Iris, I told you I had an affair with Mick—and that he once got violent." (I hate picturing the two of them together.) "What I didn't tell you is that it happened more than once." Ms. Cameron drops her voice. "It took awhile before I had the courage to break up with him."

"This shit makes me sick," Tommy mutters.

"Now Tommy," Ms. Odette says. It's obviously not his turn yet.

Mrs. Karpman is having trouble waiting for her turn too. "I knew it!" she exclaims, her voice even raspier than usual. "I could tell the first time I saw that man—"

But Ms. Cameron is not finished. "At the time, I considered going to the police, and honestly, now I wish I had. I know how seductive Mick can be, but I swear, Iris, you'll be better off without him."

Katie sputters something about wishing she had been a better friend to me. "I should have figured out what was going on," she says. "I'm so sorry I let you down, Iris."

When she's through swearing to be a better friend, Katie turns to Tommy. He looks down at his running shoes, then up at me, then over at the wall where the hole is, then back to me again. "You deserve better, Iris," he says. "I'm not saying that because you dumped me for this douchebag." Ms. Odette purses her lips when Tommy says *douchebag.* "I'm saying it because it's true."

Ms. Odette seems to be responsible for statistics. "They say"—she doesn't bother to explain who *they* is—"sixty-two percent of women have been hit, shoved or slapped. So really, Iris, when you think about it, what this man did to you and to Ms. Cameron, well, it isn't so unusual. But that doesn't make it right."

Ms. Odette hands me a brochure from her purse. There's a girl with two bruised eyes on the cover. When I push the brochure away, Ms. Odette leaves it on the coffee table, right in front of me. I turn my head so I won't have to look at the girl on the brochure. Her black eyes make me want to cry. "Iris, I want you to read this pamphlet. Then I want you to make an appointment to see me. I don't just do career counseling, you know. I have a private counseling practice too."

Mom is the only one who seems to have forgotten her lines. She's wringing her hands and making sighing noises. She's obviously working her way up to telling me something important. "Iris," she says at last, "you told me you remembered hiding in a closet when you were a little girl. I didn't want to tell you more, but now I think I have to." Mom looks over at Ms. Odette as if she needs confirmation that she is doing the right thing.

When Ms. Odette nods, Mom swallows, then goes on. "Your father and I were having a terrible fight. Our worst fight ever. I told him he had to leave. That I'd had it with his gambling. That I couldn't give him any more second chances." Mom is speaking very quietly, and I understand now that she still feels ashamed of what my dad did so many years ago. "I went to the closet for his suitcase. I didn't realize you were in there. That you'd gone to hide in the closet. And then...and then...oh, Iris!"

Everyone in the room is watching my mom's face, then my face. They are waiting for the end of her story. Only I'm the one who tells the rest, because as Mom was speaking, more of the memory came back to me. "You were shouting, and then you slammed the closet door— really hard," I say. The memory is so powerful that for a moment, I can't speak. "On my finger." Without planning to, I touch my dragon ring, twirling it slowly round my ring finger.

"Oh honey," my mom says, shutting her eyes, "I'm so sorry." When she picks up the story, her voice is barely a whisper. "We went straight to the hospital. The three of us. Your finger was badly broken." She looks at my finger, shaking her head at the memory. "It was when we were waiting in Emergency that I knew for sure it was over between your father and me. It killed me that you were hurt—and that it was my fault.

"And now"—Mom's voice breaks—"it's happened again. This man, this Mick, he's hurt you…and I wasn't there to prevent it. Honestly, Iris, I don't know what I did wrong. I just don't know. I always did my best with you."

It's Mrs. Karpman who finally tells Mom to cut it out. "Has it occurred to you, dear," she says, "that this…this situation…isn't about you? It's about Iris."

No one lets me get a word in. Maybe that's how interventions are supposed to work. Though I'm beginning to suspect this isn't exactly a textbook intervention.

I haven't always been good at standing up for myself. I realize I need to stand up for myself now. "All right then, listen up," I say to all of them, and the determination in my voice seems to catch everyone by surprise. "I need you to leave. Now. All of you."

Tommy is the first to get up from the couch.

Katie does not budge. "What about our intervention?" she asks. "Did it work?"

Mrs. Karpman pokes Katie in the elbow. "Give her time," Mrs. Karpman tries to whisper, but we can all hear her.

Mom won't stop hugging me. "I love you so much, Iris. I'm so sorry for everything. I'm sorry I wasn't there to protect you. I'm sorry I wasn't more honest. Will you at least think about what we said?"

Ms. Odette moves the brochure closer to the edge of the coffee table.

Ms. Cameron sighs dramatically when she passes the hole Mick punched in the wall.

I agree to think about what they've said.

If I didn't, they might never have left.

CHAPTER 32

"And in this harsh world draw thy breath in pain
To tell my story." —HAMLET, ACT 5, SCENE 2

I toss Ms. Odette's brochure into the recycling box, careful not to look at the battered girl on the cover. Now all that's left from the intervention are two empty pizza cartons and the smell of Ms. Cameron's patchouli perfume. Just as I'm thinking how relieved I am to be alone, someone buzzes from the lobby. I decide not to answer, but whoever it is keeps buzzing.

I drag myself to the intercom.

"Yes," I say.

"Iris, I need to come back upstairs." It's my mom. What can she want from me now?

I sigh into the intercom, then buzz her in.

"I was halfway home when I realized I had to come back," she says when we're sitting on opposite ends of Mick's leather couch. William Shakespeare has come out from under the couch, and now he leaps up onto it, settling himself on one of the zebra pillows.

"That's William Shakespeare," I tell her. "He's mine."

"He's beautiful," Mom says.

William Shakespeare purrs at the compliment.

Mom starts to reach out for my hand, then folds her hands back in her lap. "I'm sorry about tonight, Iris. I know it must have been overwhelming with all of us barging in here the way we did." She looks around the loft as if she can still see the others. I watch as her eyes linger for a moment on the print of the Bonsecours Market, which I hung back on the wall after everyone left.

"It was pretty bad."

Mom looks down at her hands. "My parents tried to talk me out of marrying your father."

"I take it you didn't listen." I don't say what I'm thinking: that if she hadn't married him, I might never have been born.

"There's something you need to understand, Iris. I was crazy in love with him." The words sound strange coming from my mom. *Crazy in love?* My mom is the least crazy person I know. She might as well have told me she is fluent in Swahili or moonlights as a belly dancer. When she looks up at me, her eyes are misty. "When we were together, the world changed for me. Things came alive in a way they never had before." Mom smiles a little at the memory. "He wasn't a bad man, Iris, but he was bad for me.

That's why I had to make him leave. And why I insisted that there be no contact between the two of you. He understood."

Because I don't know what to say, I don't say anything. My father did not abandon me. He wanted to stay in my life, but that would have been too hard for my mom. He respected her wishes. Could that have been his gift to me?

Mom gets up from the couch. "I'm going to get out of your way now," she says, tucking her purse under her arm. Before she goes, she kisses my forehead.

When I'm alone again, I go to stand by the window. I'm afraid that if I keep sitting on the couch, I'll hear the voices from the intervention in my head. From up here, the yellow lights from the streetlamps along Cavendish Boulevard make a golden chain.

I think about my mom and my dad. I try to picture them when they were my age. *Crazy in love. Not a bad man. But bad for me. I had to make him leave.*

What kind of man is Mick? I walk over to the table and pick up my cellphone. It's after 9:00 PM. Why hasn't he phoned or texted? He knows I'm waiting for news from him. Maybe the Australian cell-phone network is down. No, that's a crazy idea. He'll phone soon. I know he will.

I love him. I always will, even if we've had some rough patches. No one can ever talk me out of that. Mick has so many qualities I love and admire—he's playful, he's confident, he's creative. I want to be all those things too.

Maybe those traits are somewhere in me too, waiting to come out. Why else would they matter so much to me?

But maybe Mom, Mrs. Karpman, Ms. Cameron, Ms. Odette, Katie and Tommy are on to something. Mick's not good for me. It's not good for me that he can't control his temper. It's not good for me that he sometimes gets violent. I do worry that even if he wants to change, he won't be able to. When Mick gets in a dark mood, well, the mood is bigger than he is.

This doesn't mean I'm going to break off with him forever.

But something's changed. Something inside me feels as if it's moved, made room for something else.

For the first time, it feels like I have a choice.

If Shakespeare was right and all the world's a stage, I should be able to write my own play, shouldn't I? I should be able to come up with my own ending—and I don't want to end up like Ophelia.

Ms. Cameron had an affair with Mick, and he hit her too. Just like he must have hit Millicent.

I wish I could talk to Millicent.

Maybe I can.

I do the math in my head. It's almost 12:30 PM on Monday in Melbourne. What if I email the Victorian College of the Arts at the University of Melbourne and tell them I am trying to get in touch with someone named Millicent Temple? I compose the email message in my head before I key it in.

My name is Iris Wagner. I am trying to reach someone named Millicent Temple. I saw her in one of the promotional videos posted on your site. It is a personal matter, but please tell her it's urgent. My email is iriswagneractor@gmail.com; my phone number is 514-207-1212

I press Send before I can change my mind. There, it's done.

I go to bed before ten. I don't dream of dark forests or airports. I don't dream at all.

The vibration of the cell phone on my pillow wakes me. The first four numbers on the display are 613. Melbourne. "Mick!" I say.

"Mick?" a woman's voice asks. "Is that what this is about? Mick Horton?"

"Millicent?" My hands are shaking. I can't believe I'm talking to Millicent.

"Is this Iris?" she asks. "I got a message from you. You said it was urgent."

"Have you seen Mick? Is he okay?"

"I don't ever want to see Mick Horton again. How do you know him?"

"I—I'm his girlfriend."

I can hear Millicent suck in her breath.

"What did he do to you?" I ask. Part of me already knows.

But instead of answering, Millicent asks me a question. "Does he hit you?"

I try to say yes, but I can't.

"He must have, right? That's why you're calling me, isn't it? You need to keep away from him, Iris. I wish someone had told me that. But there was no one to tell me."

"What did he do to you?" I ask again.

I think I hear Millicent lighting up a cigarette. "He hit me—a lot. Always in my face. The last time was the worst." Millicent pauses. I hear her take a drag on her cigarette. "I'm blind in one eye."

I'm crying. But I don't know if Millicent can hear me, because she is crying too.

When I hang up, it's four in the morning, and I know I won't be able to fall back asleep. So I get out of bed, and I start packing up the stolen clothes. After school, I'll take them back to Forever 21. I'll leave them on a counter when no one's looking.

Or maybe I can find a way to tell someone what really happened—how I stole the clothes because I was afraid to stand up to my boyfriend. Because I lost myself, but now I am beginning to find myself again. If this is my story, telling the truth would make a better ending.

When the clothes are packed, I rescue Ms. Odette's brochure from the recycling box. It isn't easy, but I force my eyes to meet the girl's on the cover of the brochure. It's as if I can feel her pain. And yet she agreed to be photographed.

She must have thought it was important to let other girls know what she went through.

I am connected to that girl, and the two of us are connected to Millicent and Ms. Cameron.

I lay the brochure on the table, facing down. I'm not ready to read it yet. Maybe tomorrow I will be.

When my phone vibrates again, I can tell from the 613 number that it's another call from Melbourne. This time, it has to be Mick. For a moment, my heart leaps, but then it's as if I can feel it flutter back down in my chest.

I watch as the phone continues to vibrate on the coffee table.

Tender yourself more dearly.

Sometimes a person has to be tough on herself; other times she's got to be gentle, cut herself some slack. It depends on the situation. Sometimes being tough is the only way to tender yourself more dearly. After you've been tough, then you need to be gentle with yourself again.

I don't answer Mick's call. When the phone stops vibrating, I turn it off.

Tomorrow, I'll pack up the rest of my stuff. And I'll phone Mick and tell him what I've decided—that part of me will always love him, that I'll always be grateful for what he taught me, but that I have to let him go.

ACKNOWLEDGEMENTS

I am grateful to author Sheree Fitch, who, in a writing workshop, asked us to write the blurb for the book we most wanted to read. The blurb I wrote was very close to a synopsis of this book. Thanks also to Montreal psychotherapist Louise Dessertine and Marianopolis College counseling psychologist Lesley Lacate for helping me understand why some young women end up in abusive relationships and why it can be so difficult for them to leave. Thanks to the terrific team at Orca Book Publishers. Thanks to art director, Teresa Bubela, for the gift of a perfect cover. Deepest thanks to my editor, Sarah N. Harvey, who is both gentle and tough, for understanding how much this story means to me and for her wise guidance. Thanks to my friends: author Rina Singh, for being there for me in dark days and whose friendship has never wavered, and Viva Singer, for listening, reading and making me laugh. And thanks, as always, to the two big loves of my life: Alicia Melamed, for being my sunshine and heart's delight, and Michael Shenker, for making everything better.